# Ashes for a Crown

20250823

ISBN: 978-1-0696985-5-1

# CONTENTS

**Chapter 1.    Born from the Slag**

Hunger had always been there—not sharp and fleeting, but settled deep, permanent as the grime beneath his nails. He didn't remember a time before it. Didn't remember a mother's voice, or a home, or walls that stood straight. His world was made of crooked streets, quick hands, and eyes that watched too closely. Meals were never certain. Nothing was.

And then, one day, the world tilted.

The sky hung pale and washed out, the air thick with damp stone and brackish water. Pip worked the market streets, not like a child, but like someone who knew the rules—if you wanted something, you took it. Nobody gave freely in the Slag.

And then she was there.

She didn't belong. Not in the Slag. Not anywhere near the market. The world around her was grey and grime-streaked, but she was red. Red hair, red cloak, like a flame standing against the filth. Her boots were clean, her clothes too fine. And on her wrist—gold, gleaming, easy.

Pip moved without thinking. Small, quick, hands light as breath. She'd never notice.

But she did.

Fingers caught his wrist. Not tight, not angry, just enough to stop him cold. Pip braced for a slap, a yell, the call of a guard. None came. She just looked at him, eyes dark, measuring.

"And who is this?" she asked. Soft voice. Amused. Worse than anger. Worse than anything.

His gut clenched. A trick. Had to be. But she just let go, like it had never happened. Pip ran. Didn't look back. He rubbed his wrist where she'd touched him, his palm suddenly cold, aching for something he had never held, but knew intimately all the same.

And then she came back.

He was chewing a scrap of week-old bread, half-watching the market, when he felt it — that shift. That stillness. One second, the alley was empty. The next, she was there. Pip's breath caught. Had she always been there? He blinked. She didn't move. Just watched him, like she'd stepped in from somewhere else, somewhere he couldn't see.

She held out a cloth-wrapped bundle. "For you, Pipfinzinder."

She named him. She said it like it mattered. Like she'd carved it from the world just for him. The words settled heavy, like something she'd pulled from the air and pressed into his skin. Made him hers in a way he didn't quite understand. Had he always been that name? Or had she just decided it, and now it was real?

He shouldn't have taken the bundle. Didn't trust gifts. But when he reached out—slow, waiting for the trick—he felt warmth. And suddenly, he was starving.

She kept coming back. Never asked where he crawled from, never flinched at the stink of the Slag. Just talked to him like he was a boy, not a shadow.

The smell lingered. Parchment and oil. Clean. Warm. Wrong.

He was the Slag—grime-deep, rusted inside. She was something else. Not light exactly. Not clean. Just... different. And different was enough to hurt.

*Was he always this small? Or did he become it by wanting more?*

He never saw her coming. She was just there, pulling him out of the dark with a smile like it cost her nothing. Like he was worth it.

No one spoke to them. Guards didn't even glance their way. Pip waited for someone to drag her from him, but they never did. She was his. His alone. And he did step from the shadows. Not just hunger and cold pushing him forward. He had tasted something warm, something good, and he needed it. So, day after day, he searched the streets, the alleys, hunting the red lady.

Then she was there, and he was full again.

The last time he saw her, the day was cold and grey, thick fog rolling in off the sea. A few shadows drifted through the streets, slipping between tilted houses. Pip curled in a corner, scraps pulled tight around his frame, shaking from the chill. He must have closed his eyes, because suddenly she was kneeling before him, brushing dirt from his cheek like she didn't mind the filth, like he was something more than a half-starved thing wrapped in rags.

From her sleeve — like magic — she pulled something that caught the light. Pressed it into his palm.

A coin. Firelite-flecked gold. Like bottled sunlight.

"I think you should have this, Pip," she said, smiling. "Something of your own."

Pip had never owned anything before. His dirty fingers reached out, toward her face. She didn't flinch. But then — something inside him twisted. Something he hadn't known was there, hadn't known could move. It happened in an instant. One second, she was there, red hair falling over him like fire. Then —

A pull. A hollowing. The air stretched thin, like the world had exhaled and forgotten how to draw breath. Cold slithered under his skin — not the kind that came from wind or damp, but something deeper, something that took. The coin in his palm felt heavier, like it had stolen something unseen. A whisper brushed against his thoughts — too faint to name — then was gone, leaving only silence.

Her smile faltered. Her eyes dulled, like something inside her had dimmed. A shiver ran through her, a stumble, like she'd lost something without knowing what it was.

Whatever she had been… faded.

Pip's breath hitched.

Her eyes passed right through him, empty, like looking at a street with no one standing there. Like he wasn't real.

Panic clawed up his ribs. She had always seen him. Always. But now — now she didn't. He reached, but she was already stepping back. The scent of honey and firelight slipped away, fading like warmth from cold fingers.

Then she turned and walked into the fog.

Gone.

No sound but the hush of the sea, the shifting silt beneath his feet. No trace but the damp where she'd stood, the last curl of her scent bleeding into the rain. Like she'd never been there at all.

He never saw her again.

No one spoke of her. No one remembered her. Pip asked, once, if anyone had seen the woman with red hair. They only stared at him, blank, waiting for the punchline. Like he'd made her up. Like she'd only ever existed for him, pulled from the fog for a moment and then swallowed back into it.

He didn't cry. Couldn't. The world was cold again, sharp-edged, but tears weren't something he knew.

That night, he found a wrecked hovel and made it his. A narrow, broken thing wedged between two leaning walls, damp stone at his back, just enough space to curl into. There, he turned the coin over in his fingers. Again. And again. And again. Until the edges burned warm against his skin.

**Chapter 2.     Where Knives Rule**

---

Where the Bay of Viridos met land, Port Gatos sprawled—fat, cracked, rotting at the seams. It had crawled up the broken back of a mountain that had tried to rise and failed, just like everything else here. The biggest port in the west, it stank of salt, sweat, and old blood. A place where a man had to keep his head down and his knife close. The land was cracked and uneven, streets twisting like a rat's warren. Buildings leaned like drunks, some propped up with beams, others waiting to collapse. You learned early which doors to avoid, which streets had eyes in the dark.

Pip didn't much care about the High Ward. That was where the merchant princes and coin-counters lived, behind thick walls and iron gates. They had their own way of bleeding people dry, and it didn't involve knives in the street. Two-Fingers ran things up there, quiet and careful, but that world wasn't for Pip. Too many rules, too many people who thought themselves untouchable. He only knew what mattered: if a job took you past those walls, you were either worth something or already dead.

The Low Quarter turned mean when the sun dropped. Sweat and piss and rot in the air. Alleys cut like blades, waiting for someone to trip. Blacktooth ran it. You owed him, whether you knew it or not. He made sure every pickpocket, every beggar, every poor bastard trying to scrape by, paid their share. And if they didn't, well — no one had to wonder what happened next.

Down by the bay, the Waterfront heaved with ships, warehouses, and men who measured their days in coin and curses. Salt and fish stung the air, thick as the stink of pitch and sweat. Rat-Eye ran the docks. Nothing moved in or out without her say-so, and if someone got greedy, they were taking their last breath before sunrise. Pip had seen it happen. Quick, quiet, and straight into the water.

To the west, past where the city bothered pretending it was still a city, the Slag spread out in filth and firelight. The land sagged and crumbled, houses built on bad ground, sinking bit by bit. The deeper in you went, the worse it got — until the streets just ended, swallowed up like they were never there. Ruined stone, broken men, and the kind of dark that swallowed people whole. That was where The Knife ruled. His Butchers didn't come with threats or warnings. They waited, watched. Listened. When they moved, the world went quiet. Problems disappeared. People did too. Pip knew better than to ask where they went. If you had to ask, you weren't meant to know.

At the centre of it all sat Duke Cassian Sargo, the Red Knives' Guildmaster. Pip didn't know much about him. Didn't need to. The man had built himself into something untouchable, not by being the biggest or the strongest, but by making himself necessary.

Everyone needed him for something, and that meant no one dared take him out. Pip figured that was the best kind of power to have—the kind that didn't need showing off. Sargo didn't need to raise his voice or swing a blade. That's what his Quartermasters were for. They handled the bloodletting. He just sat back and made sure they never got ideas above their place.

Pip had spent years figuring out the real rules of Gatos, the ones no one wrote down, the ones that mattered. He'd learned them the hard way.

The Knife had noticed him early, like a butcher picking out a pig worth fattening. In the Slag, getting noticed by The Knife meant one of two things: you worked for him, or you ended up somewhere no one would find you.

Pip had been invited to keep breathing.

Darrik had been the one to show him the ropes. Not out of kindness—there was none of that in this work—but because someone had to. A new hand needed shaping, and Darrik liked things done right. He didn't expect Pip to last. Most didn't. But after the first job, he'd started watching him differently—like a man who'd lit a fire and wasn't sure what he'd set burning.

Debt collection was a trade. You told them what they owed, gave them a chance to pay, made an example if they didn't. Kept it clean when you could, messy when you had to. Pip didn't do messy. But he didn't do clean, either. He worked in that space between—quick, quiet, final. No threats, no shouting, no wasted movement. Just the blade, the target, and the moment they realized too late that the knife was already moving.

Even Darrik had learned to tread careful around him. He never said it outright, but Pip caught it in the way his eyes flicked to his hands before speaking, the way his tone changed when giving instructions. A warning about breaking kneecaps had ended with a man screaming on the ground, his leg shattered before he'd even had time to beg. Darrik had looked at him a beat too long, then muttered, "You're cold, kid." He never made that mistake again. These days, when he told Pip to do something, it was already decided. No room for hesitation. No second guessing.

It worked well enough. They weren't friends—Pip didn't have those, didn't need them—but he trusted Darrik to be what he was. Straightforward. No tricks, no double-dealing. He did the work, took his cut, and didn't waste time with anything that didn't matter. He didn't flinch at blood, didn't hesitate when a job needed doing, and most importantly, he never asked questions after it was done.

They passed the time easy enough. Some nights were quick—cracked ribs, stolen coin, a few parting threats, and they were gone. Other nights were slow, long stretches of waiting, letting fear do the work before they ever raised a hand. Darrik filled the space with talk. Not important things, just the usual—complaints, old stories, little scraps of a past that Pip never asked about. He didn't expect Pip to answer, which suited him fine. When Darrik talked, Pip listened. And when he didn't, that was fine too.

The Butchers' Guildhouse squatted in the Slag like an old mutt too stubborn to die, its bones warped, its hide patched where time and trouble had left their marks. The place breathed with watching eyes, men moving slow, careful, like they knew the walls had ears. Words were worth more unspoken than said. Knives got checked more often than coin. Survival meant knowing when to talk and when to disappear. The air inside sat thick—sweat, smoke, the sour tang of spilled ale long soaked into the wood. The floors groaned underfoot, uneven and pitted, worn down by too many boots, too many bodies hitting the ground. A rusted iron stove in the corner gave off a dull heat, its soot-streaked pipe winding through the ceiling. Up in the rafters, knives stuck where they'd been thrown and left, handles jutting out like broken teeth.

Pip and Darrik were killing time, rolling bones over a battered table in the back. Darrik tapped the dice against the wood, watching Pip like he was waiting for something interesting. He was always half-amused, half-calculating, like he couldn't decide if Pip was worth trusting or just fun to watch.

"You ever gonna bet something real?" Darrik asked,

tossing the dice. A six and a three.

Pip barely looked. "No."

Darrik snorted. "Figured."

The game wasn't about winning. It was about filling the spaces between jobs. Keeping their hands busy, keeping their thoughts from circling back to things best left alone. Too much quiet made a man start thinking, and thinking led to doubts. The dice gave them something simple, something that didn't ask for anything but the roll.

The door swung open. The Knife's voice cut through the low murmur of the room.

"You two. Now."

Pip glanced up, already pushing back his chair. Darrik sighed, stretching. "Should've known. You only ever call when we're busy."

The Knife didn't answer, just jerked his head toward the back hall.

Noose Varik was already there when they stepped in, arms crossed, lantern light cutting hard lines across his face. He never looked at Pip unless he had to, and when he did, it was with the kind of disgust a man saved for things that crawled under floorboards.

Suits me fine, Pip thought.

Noose was close to The Knife, one of the few men the Quartermaster trusted outright. Smart. Careful. Good at making people disappear without a mess.

He trusted iron more than people, and his desk had more blades than papers. Rumor said he filed his nails with a sliver of bone—his own, once shattered in a fight.

The Knife didn't trust Pip. He gave him work, gave him orders, but trust? No. That was something else entirely. Pip saw it in the way The Knife looked at him too long sometimes, like he was waiting for something to make sense. Like Pip was a puzzle he didn't remember buying, and now it was missing half the pieces.

The Knife leaned forward; hands flat on the desk. "Warehouse job," he said, voice steady, cold. "Shipment's coming in. Needs holding until it's moved."

Pip kept quiet. Darrik asked the question.

"Where?"

"White Hall. The Hollow."

Nobody named The Hollow. It just got called that. A place where the ground swallowed things—buildings, people, memories. Some parts of the Slag had bad foundations. This stretch had none at all. It took what it wanted, left the rest tilting on the edge, waiting to follow.

The Butchers had a warehouse there. Not much of one. Looked like it was waiting to die, leaning too far to one side, its beams warped, half its lower level collapsed into the dark below. The place stank of old wood and damp rot, like something had been left to spoil and nobody cared enough to move it.

Nobody watched places in The Hollow. No one figured they were worth the trouble. But The Knife had decided this one was good enough for a shipment that couldn't be seen.

Something twisted in Pip's gut. Not the docks. Not a guarded storehouse. Just a broken hulk rotting in the Slag, where the earth swallowed things whole. Didn't sit right.

The Knife must've caught something in his face, because his gaze flicked to Pip. "You got a problem with that?"

Pip didn't answer. Didn't have to.

The Knife held his gaze for a second, then turned to Noose. "Rat-Eye might find herself missing a shipment tonight."

Noose nodded.

That got Darrik's attention. His eyes flicked to Pip, like he expected a reaction. Pip didn't give him one.

Everyone knew The Knife and Rat-Eye didn't get along. Too much bad blood, too much waiting for an excuse. The Knife never wasted breath on her without spitting after. Taking a shipment from her — that wasn't just business. That was setting a fire just to watch it spread.

Darrik frowned, but didn't ask. Didn't need to. He was thinking the same thing Pip was: What's in the shipment?

Pip already knew. He'd heard The Knife and Noose talking when they thought no one was listening. Duke Sargo was expecting something from Tahl'Vareth. Not just coin, not just trade goods — something personal. Something important enough that Rat-Eye was handling it herself. Important enough that The Knife wanted her to fail.

And The Knife had told Noose he "better not screw it up."

"Why not bring it here?" Pip asked.

The room turned to him. He didn't talk much. Made people listen when he did.

The Knife's face twisted. "Because here's the first place she'd look, you idiot! You stick to sticking things and let me do the thinking."

Pip shifted, tilting his weight just enough to seem restless. Unimpressed.

The Knife watched him a beat longer, then moved on. "Now you get why it's being kept in the White

Hall. No one would think to look there."

Darrik grunted, accepting it. Pip wasn't so sure.

He thought about it. How stealing from Rat-Eye could push The Knife up the ladder. How if Pip were doing it, he'd make it look like an inside job, or like someone got sloppy. But then — why not bring it to the Guildhouse? Unless this wasn't just about making Rat-Eye look like a fool. No one would think to look there. Or no one would think to question what happened there. A shipment hidden in a place already half-swallowed by the earth. If something went wrong, there wouldn't be much left to find. And maybe that was the plan.

Darrik let a breath out like it owed him money, scratching at his jaw. "And if someone does show up?

The Knife barely looked up. "Then make sure they never leave."

# Chapter 3.    The Gatos Cage

Aieria stood at the window, her fingers curled into the thick fabric of the curtain, its heavy weight pooling around her knuckles. The air was damp with the scent of rain, the distant tang of saltwater carried in from the docks. She peered down at the streets below, watching as figures moved through the murky light, their steps hurried, their heads bowed against the drizzle. A chill crept through the wooden floorboards beneath her feet, seeping into her bones. The streets of Port Gatos stretched below, a restless sprawl of filth and motion. Voices hummed through the damp air, mingling with the distant crash of waves against the docks, the ceaseless rhythm of a city that never truly slept. It was another day, indistinguishable from the last.

Days into weeks. Weeks into months.

Time bled together in this dim little room, the walls pressing in, thick with the scent of old wood, candle smoke, and the lingering salt of the sea.

Waiting. But for what?

"You must allow yourself time to heal, your Grace," Keal had said, with perfect inflection of caring and duty. It was a lie.

"Healing?" She laughed softly, bitterly. "Healing implies I could return to what I was. This," she said, waving bitterly to her back, "is clearly beyond restoration, Kael."

But Kael's expression remained unchanged. Careful. Neutral. Giving her nothing.

Time stretched endlessly, the days blurring together in a slow haze, offering little solace or change. And no salve could restore what had been lost—her wings, her crown, the life she had once known. She had once soared above the world, weightless and powerful, but now she was grounded, tethered to a fate she had never imagined. The loss was not just physical; it was a hollowing of her essence, an unraveling of everything she had once been. Healing felt distant, unattainable—only the weight of loss remained, pressing down with every step forward, no matter how carefully taken.

It was true that the small pathetic lumps between her shoulders no longer bled. But the absence was a wound all its own. And her physical mutilation was only part of her injury. Severed wings she could hide beneath clothing, carefully draped to create the illusion that she was whole. Other wounds carved deeper; in places no bandage could reach. In the stillness of night she ached, phantom wings curling, stretching—an absence more painful than presence. She loathed them. She loathed herself.

Aieria had carefully wrapped herself in layers of fabric, arranging the folds to obscure the truth of what she had become. Her fingers trembled when they traced the ruined flesh, the grotesque remains of what had once been beautiful. She had been a Queen. A daughter of the skies. A ruler whose very bloodline was meant to soar above the world. Now she was nothing but a mockery of it—a fallen thing.

Kael came and went like a shadow. He never knocked, never announced himself. One moment the room would be empty, and the next, he would be there, slipping through the door, unseen and unheard by the rest of the world. He had always moved like that, even in the Sky Kingdom. He had been one of the kingdom's best, after all. Kael said little. Too little. He never lied—but he never said who he answered to, either. Even now, Aieria wasn't sure if he guarded her… or kept her.

And Seraphina. Mother. Slain at Immaris. Aieria had spent her life caught between admiration and fear, yearning for her approval while dreading her sharp tongue and sharper mind. Even now, in death, Seraphina's shadow loomed large—her expectations, her manipulations, the weight of a rule that had never truly been Aieria's to claim. And yet, despite it all, she mourned.

Aieria pressed her forehead to the cool glass, the weight of the thought settling into her ribs. The Queen Regent had been a force of will, a mind sharper than any blade. Aieria had loved her. Feared her. Had spent a lifetime struggling beneath her shadow. And now she was gone.

The world she had once ruled had been devoured by fire and darkness. The Aier were no more. What was once a proud and luminous kingdom had been reduced to ash, its people hunted, its cities broken. The armies of light, once a force to challenge the heavens, had been shattered like brittle glass beneath the Infernii's relentless advance. Their numbers had never been enough. Their faith had never been enough. The great banners of Aier had been torn down, their golden threads unraveling into the mud, their radiant crests trampled and ruined.

Aeon still fought, leading the remnants of the Aierian forces in a desperate war against an enemy that did not tire, did not falter. Aetherion still stood, a shining beacon of resistance, its towers still piercing the heavens. But the high cities were besieged, cut off from one another, their supplies dwindling, their strength bleeding away. They clung to the sky, but for how much longer? The lower cities had already fallen, their firelite streets corrupted with shadow, their people enslaved or worse. The Infernii did not simply conquer; they defiled, twisted everything in their wake, leaving behind only horror and ruin.

And at the centre of it all, like a black wound in the heart of the world, loomed Antima.

Antima had not merely been corrupted—it had withered, its firelite core flickering as it failed to hold the weight of the city aloft. Once, it had floated high among the celestial cities, untouchable, a beacon of

Aierian might. But Balog had poisoned its essence, unraveling the firelite's radiance thread by thread. With a shuddering groan, it had slowly descended — a slow, inexorable sinking, the city drifting lower with each passing day through the clouds, like a drowning leviathan. Now, it sat hunched on the ground, like a blackened spire driven deep into the earth, its form twisted and lifeless, a mockery of its former grandeur. It was no longer a city of the heavens. It was a husk, a festering wound at the heart of the world, Balog's dark citadel, Korr-Azûn.

Her hands clenched into fists, the curtain bunching beneath her fingers.

Kael had told her all of it. Piece by piece, bringing whispers of the outside world into this small room, offering scraps of knowledge as if they could sustain her.

"There are those who are still loyal to you," he had said, his voice low, measured.

She had turned to him then, searching his expression, but he had only met her gaze with that same quiet certainty.

"Your survival is enough for now."

But it wasn't. Not for her.

She was tired of waiting. Of sitting in the dark, listening to the world crumble, watching the pieces fall while she did nothing.

Her fingers loosened, the heavy curtain slipping from her grip. The streets below blurred; the movement of the city lost to the storm inside her.

Survival was not enough.

Not anymore.

The Brass Griffin Inn was neither grand nor squalid, standing on the quiet side of the Low Quarter. It was the kind of place that earned no second glance, where no one asked questions so long as the coin was good. Aieria had lived within its walls for months, hidden in plain sight. Kael had purchased it outright, replacing its key staff with people who would keep their mouths shut—people who, ideally, still held some loyalty to the Sky Kingdom. She knew that was the idea, at least.

But in truth, the inn did not belong to her. It belonged to Kael. And Kael answered to no one but himself.

Everything that surrounded her—the room, the bed, the food, the careful protection that encircled this quiet, unremarkable place—was bought with the Crown's money. Her money. And yet, none of it was controlled by her. It was a truth she had swallowed for months, but tonight, it burned on her tongue.

Outside her door, her ever-present warden stood guard. Indaros Vato. A man with the hardened look of a soldier long accustomed to violence, the kind of man who had made his peace with killing. He was older than Kael, built broad and solid, with the quiet patience of someone who expected trouble and was confident in his ability to end it. His sword rarely left his side, and Aieria had little doubt he could gut a man before his opponent had a chance to reach for a blade.

She had no hope of slipping past him.

Nor past the inn's other workers, who should have been loyal to her but, in the end, were paid by Kael. She was their Queen in name, but Kael held their loyalty in his coin-purse. To them, she was not their ruler. She was their responsibility.

That left only one way out.

She turned to the window, drawing back the wooden shutter just enough to peer into the night. Her breath caught in her throat, hesitation clawing at the edges of her resolve. The air beyond was thick with the scent of rain-soaked stone, the distant murmur of the city whispering of freedom, of danger. For months, she had been caged, her every movement dictated by others. The thought of slipping away, of reclaiming even a fragment of control, sent a shiver down her spine. A narrow ledge ran just beneath the sill, stone worn smooth by time and rain. It extended to the building's side, where a drainpipe clung to the wall like an iron spine, bolted in place but rusting in spots. The drop to the alley below was far, but not lethal—so long as she didn't misstep. Beyond that, she could see the rooftops sloping gently downward toward the main street. If she moved carefully, she could make her way along them, find an easier descent, and disappear into the city's tangled veins.

She exhaled, steadying herself. Kael would call this reckless. Indaros would see it as a risk not worth taking. But she was tired of being told what was best for her. Tired of waiting for permission that would never come.

Aieria had never had to sneak before. She had never had to run. Even now, her fingers hesitated against the windowsill, her body still expecting the weight of wings to carry her down. But there were no wings, no effortless descent into the night. Only the stones beneath her feet, the cool air against her skin, and the city waiting below.

She swung her leg over the sill and stepped onto the ledge. For a moment, she hesitated, the wind tugging at her clothes, the height below a stark reminder of how far she had fallen. Her foot slipped—just an inch—but her breath seized. The stones were slick from the evening mist. No wings. No second chances. There was no turning back now—only forward, only down. With a steadying breath, she pressed herself against the stone, gripping the edge with fingers that trembled despite her resolve.

And the city swallowed her.

As night closed around her, the city no longer felt like a cage but a chessboard. Her wounds were deep, yes, but deeper still was her resolve to use them — to weaponize what was left, rather than mourn what was gone.

**Chapter 4.    The Cost of Freedom**

Aieria moved with a sure-footed grace, her fingers dancing over the rugged brickwork, her bare soles pressing lightly against the ledge. Her weight — so much less than it once was — made the ascent effortless, almost instinctive. Aieria was built lighter than a human, her limbs leaner, her bones subtly finer, giving her a natural buoyancy that let her move with uncanny ease. To her surprise, she adapted quickly to the climb, her body seeming to remember a time when the sky had been hers.

She had escaped her cage.

The city sprawled before her, a patchwork of crooked streets and bustling life, a great unruly thing that never quite settled. The Low Quarter, with its narrow alleys and weather-worn facades, was alive with the scent of sea brine and baking bread, the cheerful clamour of voices rising and falling like the tide. Aieria walked amongst it all with an ease that felt foreign, yet deliciously right. She had no attendants, no trailing guards, no watchful eyes to weigh her down. No title to carry like a stone about her neck. For the first time, she wasn't a queen, a prisoner, a burden. Just… herself.

And God, it felt good.

She followed the lively pulse of the city to the market, where colour and chaos reigned supreme.

Stalls bristled with ripe fruit, bolts of vivid cloth, fresh fish still glistening from the morning's catch. The air was thick with the perfume of spices and roasting meats, rich and tantalizing. The sheer vibrancy of it all thrilled her; she allowed herself to be swept along by the current of traders and customers, by the playful haggling and bursts of laughter.

Her fingers curled around the gold coin in her pocket, and she felt a flicker of amusement. She had lifted it from Kael's carefully guarded stores, an act of quiet rebellion that sent a spark of satisfaction through her. It was hers anyway, wasn't it? The wealth of the Sky Kingdom, siphoned into careful hands. What harm was there in reclaiming just a small piece?

She approached a vendor, drawn by the tantalizing scent of sizzling skewers. The man behind the stall was broad-shouldered, his apron well-worn, his beard peppered with grey. She placed the coin on the counter with the casual air of someone accustomed to being served.

The vendor froze.

His eyes flickered from her to the coin, his fingers hesitating before he picked it up, turning it in the light. "This—this is Sky Kingdom gold."

Aieria blinked, momentarily wrong-footed. "Yes?"

He exhaled slowly. "I don't have enough change for

this, miss."

Aieria frowned. She hadn't even considered that. She hadn't thought of coin at all, really — of how strange it might be to carry relics of a fallen kingdom in a place like this. "I don't have silver," she admitted, suddenly feeling a little foolish.

The vendor considered her for a long moment, then shook his head with a bemused chuckle. "Take it," he said, sliding the skewer toward her. "No charge."

She opened her mouth to protest, but he merely smiled. "You've given me a story to tell. That's worth more than a few coppers."

Aieria accepted the food with a small, genuine smile. "Thank you."

The first bite was divine — perfectly spiced, with just the right char. She savoured it slowly, letting the flavours unfurl across her tongue, letting the moment stretch. She was happy. Truly happy. She wandered toward the docks, the taste of the skewer still fresh in her mouth, the sunlight catching in the rippling water. The ships bobbed in their moorings, grand vessels with sails furled, their wooden hulls whispering of places far beyond this city. She could go anywhere. Become anyone. The thought curled through her like a warm breeze, lifting her spirits with the promise of possibility.

But the day was waning. She turned back toward the Brass Griffin Inn, her pace unhurried, reluctant to return to the world she knew.

Then the feeling came.

A prickling at the back of her neck. A shift in the air. A presence. She glanced over her shoulder. A figure loitered too long at the edge of the street before slipping into the crowd.

Aieria quickened her pace.

The footsteps behind her did the same. The buildings seemed to press closer, the once-welcoming streets now narrow and unfamiliar. The inn wasn't far. Just a little further. She broke into a jog, her pulse quickening. Ahead, a figure stepped out from the shadows. Another behind her. Aieria's breath caught. They moved in slowly, with the kind of confidence that spoke of experience.

Aieria's back met the cool stone of the wall, her heartbeat a wild, frantic thing. Kael had warned her about the city, about its dangers. Indaros had kept her caged for a reason. And she—she had been so very foolish.

"Easy now," one of them said, his voice almost conversational.

Her throat tightened, a painful knot forming as her breath hitched. Every instinct screamed at her to move, to fight, to do something—but she was frozen, paralyzed beneath the crushing weight of fear and realization. A hand grabbed her arm, too tight.

Another slipped into her cloak. The jolt of fingers against her ribs. She tried to twist, but the alley was too narrow. Their breath smelled like wine and meat and sweat.

They took everything.

The world was silent in their wake. Her breath came in ragged gasps as she sank down to sit against the cold, damp stones. She hadn't fought. She hadn't screamed. That, perhaps, was the worst part. There had been a moment—a single, fleeting moment—when she could have acted. But she had hesitated. And in that hesitation, she had lost everything.

She stared blankly at the uneven stones. The city's noise had faded, distant and blurred, as though it belonged to another world. She could still feel their hands on her, rough and unapologetic, lingering too long. A shudder crawled through her, a feeling of filth she could never scrub away. For a long time, she remained there, numb, her body refusing to move, her mind retreating somewhere cold and unreachable. She had escaped the cage. But she hadn't escaped being prey.

"Miss? Are you alright?"

She flinched at the stranger's voice, recoiling from the gentle hand that reached toward her. She looked up. A rough face. Kind, concerned eyes. Humiliation washed over her like a wave.

"Thank you. I'm fine. Just resting a moment." A

smile, brittle and false, smoothed onto her lips.

"You sure? Alright then."

The stranger hesitated but then walked on, leaving her alone with her shame.

Relief. Relief that she didn't have to speak of it, didn't have to force words past the knot in her throat, didn't have to see pity in a stranger's gaze.

She took a steadying breath. And stood.

She had thought she was free.

*She wasn't free. She was just alone.*

# Chapter 5.    White Hall

Fog rolled in thick from the sea, swallowing sound, swallowing light, turning the world into shifting grey. White Hall sat in it like a carcass, damp stone sweating salt, wood sagging under the weight of rot. The whole place smelled like things left too long in the dark. A hole gaped in the floor where the ground had given up. Another in the ceiling, twenty feet up, framing the sky like a blind eye. You could fall or you could climb, but either way, you weren't getting out that way. That left two doors. The front — wood, crooked, hanging off its frame. The back — iron, rust-bitten, still holding. A place like this didn't keep its secrets for long.

Sargo's crates sat too neat, too obvious, dead centre in the hall. Bait.

Darrik leaned against a beam, arms crossed, while Pip paced, the Crooked Dagger cold against his chest. He felt it there — more than steel, more than weight. A thing that whispered when nothing else did. Pip ignored it. Tried to. The fog outside stretched silence thin, turned nothing into something. Then — footsteps. More than one set. Darrik straightened. The front doors creaked open. Fog curled around the figures stepping through.

Rat-Eye.

She moved like someone who had never been told

no. Behind her, four men fanned out, relaxed, ready. Gull, sharp-eyed and smirking. Marik Thorn, fat on bribes, puffed up like a man who thought coin made him untouchable. Salt, professional, quiet, the kind who made problems vanish. And Redwake, a pirate who carried his reputation in the way he moved — like he'd killed enough men to stop counting.

Darrik exhaled, slow, rolling his shoulders before straightening. The air shifted. Too many bodies. Too still. Pip had already faded back into the shadows, the fog outside blurring the edges, making it easy to disappear.

Rat-Eye stepped forward, all confidence, all ease. She knew Darrik. Knew he wouldn't start something he couldn't finish.

A slow smile. "Those crates are mine."

Darrik tilted his head. "That so?"

Rat-Eye's men spread out, closing the space with the kind of lazy assurance that came from never expecting a real fight. "We're taking them. I'll deal with The Knife myself. No need for this to get messy." She flicked a hand toward Darrik like he was an afterthought. "No need for you to die."

Darrik's sword cleared leather with an easy scrape, steel whispering sharp through the quiet. "I'd hope not."

Then — from outside — a heavy thud. A shift.

Something dragged, something weighty scraping wood.

Rat-Eye's gaze flicked toward the door. Tension coiled in her frame, her sharp eyes cutting toward Salt. "Salt. Check on Talla."

Salt strode forward, grabbed the handle, yanked. It rattled, but didn't move. He frowned, pulled harder. Barred from the outside. Fog curled through the gaps, thick and creeping, but beyond that—nothing.

He peered through, called. "Talla?"

No answer.

Rat-Eye's fingers flexed. Pip saw it—how her weight shifted, the slow drift of her hand toward her hilt, the twitch of her jaw as she processed. Something was wrong.

"What's going on?" Her voice sharpened, slicing into the quiet.

Darrik rolled one shoulder, slow. "You tell me. Your woman's the one who's gone quiet."

Rat-Eye didn't buy it. Pip saw that too. The way she held still, like a coiled wire waiting to snap.

"It's a trap," she said, flat. "Salt, get that door open."

Salt cursed, braced himself, and threw his weight against the doors. They didn't budge.

"Redwake," Rat-Eye snapped. "Check the back. Report."

The pirate grunted and moved, his gait rolling like a man who'd lived half his life on a deck. Pip watched him go, footsteps soundless against damp wood, slipping toward the rear exit.

Rat-Eye's focus swung back to Darrik. Her smile was gone. "Kill him."

Gull and Thorn stepped forward, easy, casual. Men who'd done this before. Gull had his gutting knives, two sharp crescents ready to open skin. Thorn carried a short sword, worn but wicked. Darrik exhaled, slow, waiting. His blade hung loose in his grip, but Pip saw the shift in his stance. He was measuring. Weighing.

Did The Knife really think they could take two on four? Or had he just signed their deaths? Pip made his decision. Redwake would be a problem. He moved slow, careful, steady through the fog-thick space. The Crooked Dagger sat in his grip. He hadn't drawn it. His stomach twisted. He hadn't reached for it. No time to think about that. No time for anything but the blade, the mark, the job. Redwake first. Then hide it before anyone saw.

Behind him, steel clashed.

Redwake had one foot near the back hall—nothing but splintered beams and open air now—when Pip reached him. The pirate turned, sensing something.

Too late. Pip drove the dagger in, just below the ribs. Not clean. Not instant. Redwake gasped, wet and choking. Pip twisted. The pirate sagged, fingers weakly grabbing at Pip's wrist, but the strength had already gone out of him. A strangled, gurgling sound tore from his throat—too loud. Too desperate. Then he crumpled into the dark.

Rat-Eye's sharp eyes snapped to him. "He's got his little goblin in the back!" she snarled, then barked, "Salt, get that door open!"

Salt cursed, fighting with the front door.

Darrik staggered, blood dark on his side. Thorn was hurt too, his stance off, but not enough. Pip darted forward, looking for an opening. Thorn spotted him first. He pivoted, leaving Gull to finish Darrik.

And then everything unraveled.

Thorn came fast—faster than he looked. Steel hissed past Pip's ear. Another swing—wide, heavy—Pip ducked low, too slow. Pain licked across his shoulder as leather gave way. He staggered back, breath sharp, blood hot. Thorn lunged again. Pip twisted, slipping free by instinct, not skill. One step slower and that blade would've opened him stem to stern. Thorn pressed harder. Pip staggered back, barely catching a downward chop that sent pain screaming up his arm. The bastard fought like a hammer, brute force behind every strike. Pip feinted left, twisted right, but Thorn read it. A boot slammed into his ribs.

Pain cracked through him. He hit the floor hard, rolling just as Rat-Eye's stiletto flashed for his throat. The blade skidded off his shoulder instead, shallow but searing. His roll tangled her legs. She stumbled, balance lost, crashing back into Thorn.

"Get the hell out of the way!" Thorn snapped, stepping wide to keep from tripping.

Pip didn't waste it. He scrambled up, breath ragged, ribs screaming. Thorn was already coming. Fast. Heavy. Every strike forced Pip back, knocking him toward the yawning hole in the floor. Another swing—Pip ducked too late. The tip of Thorn's blade slashed across his forearm. Blood slicked his grip. Thorn grinned, sensing the kill. He lunged; blade aimed for Pip's throat—

Pip wasn't there.

He dropped low, twisting sideways at the last second. Thorn's weight carried forward. A bad step. A shift. His boot skidded on splintered wood. Pip saw it. The opening. The moment of tilt before the fall. He slipped left, quick as breath, and slammed his dagger into the meat of Thorn's thigh. Felt it punch through muscle. Cut deep.

Thorn roared, twisting as he swung. The blade caught Pip's cheekbone—shallow, burning. He barely registered it. Thorn's boot hit splintered wood. For a breath, he teetered, arms flailing. The moment stretched, caught between one heartbeat and the next. Then the weight tipped. He vanished into the dark.

A sickening crunch below. Silence.

Then—

"Fire!"

Rat-Eye's voice cut through the air, sharp, urgent. Flames licked at the outer walls, turning fog to glowing embers. Smoke coiled thick, churning through the broken rafters, choking the sky. The air thickened—burning wood, salt, rot. The fire was everywhere, swallowing the warped planks, heat swelling through the walls. Salt let the door burn. Took his place beside her, face carved in firelight. Gull and Darrik staggered over, both worse for wear—Darrik's side dark with blood, Gull clutching one arm, face tight with pain.

Rat-Eye barely moved, watching the flames with the steady gaze of someone taking stock. When she spoke, her voice was calm, clinical. "None of us were meant to leave."

Pip steadied himself. Ribs aching. Sweat slick on his back.

Rat-Eye exhaled, low. "Sargo let slip to the Quartermasters that something precious to him was arriving at the docks. Asked me to make sure it was delivered safely." She watched the fire chew through the doorframe, the edges curling like paper. "I wondered if it was a test. Or if he meant for blood." She flicked her wrist, dismissing the thought. "Doesn't matter. We're here because The Knife saw a chance—one too tempting to pass up. Undermine me. Dispose of me, if he could."

Pip swallowed. The pieces fell, weighted dice clicking into place.

Salt's jaw clenched. "So, he stacked the deck."

Rat-Eye nodded. "Shipment lands. Vanishes. Same day." Rat-Eye's voice was flat, but heat simmered beneath. "Then one of mine overhears where it's stashed. Right here." She nodded toward the crates. "Too neat." Her gaze cut to Darrik. "You knew whose goods they were. But you didn't expect *me*." A pause. "Means your boss didn't want you ready. Just wanted you in the way."

She glanced at the door, lips thinning. "Probably had Choke take care of Talla. She would have seen them coming, called the warning."

Pip nodded. He'd seen Choke at work. Almost as good as Pip at moving in the dark. And once the wire was around your neck, that was it.

The fire crackled, its glow sharp in Rat-Eye's eyes. She stepped toward Darrik, voice even, like she was turning a thought over in her head. "Bar the door. Burn us alive. A derelict warehouse in the Slag goes up—no one asks questions. Just another Noose accident." A flicker of something humorless crossed her lips. "That about right?"

The heat pressed in. Flames licked through gaps in the rotted walls, curling around beams that had barely been holding the place up. Smoke thickened, swallowing the rafters, choking out the stars.

Darrik shot Pip a look. "We need a way out."

Rat-Eye smiled — barely. "First thing you've said all night that I agree with."

A sharp crack split the air as the front door buckled, flames devouring the wood. The heat surged, sucking the air from Pip's lungs. Sweat slicked his back, burning in every cut. Rat-Eye didn't flinch. "If you want to live," she said, "you're going to have to stop trying to kill each other." She turned that sharp gaze on them. "And you two — your careers with the Butchers are done. Even if you survive, you're dead men." She let that settle. Then, with a slight tilt of her head, she added, "So here's my offer. We get out of here; you work for me. And we all get to kill The Knife."

Darrik met her eyes. Breathing hard. Didn't argue.

Rat-Eye pivoted. "Back door. Now."

Smoke churned overhead, ash falling in thick, burning flakes. The iron door loomed ahead, rust-bitten but solid. Rat-Eye ran a hand over the warped edges of the wall and gave a sharp shake of her head.

"Forget the door. Take the wall. Knock it loose, the weight does the work."

She looked to Salt and Darrik. "Together."

They moved into place. Rat-Eye held up a hand before they started. "The Knife's men will be waiting. Be ready."

Salt and Darrik nodded. Then braced themselves—and drove forward. The first impact rattled through the structure, dust and splinters raining down. The second sent a deep groan through the frame. The fire surged, swallowing more of the walls, pressing close.

"One more," Rat-Eye barked.

They slammed into it again. Wood snapped. Iron buckled. The door tore loose, dragging half the wall with it. Cold night air rushed in—tainted with smoke, but better than burning alive. They stumbled out.

The fog was gone, burned away by the fire's heat. In its place stood shadows. Waiting. Noose. Behind him, five enforcers—The Knife's best. Hollow, silent as a grave. Choke, flexing his fingers, already looking for a neck to squeeze. Split, blade restless, eyes hungrier than his gut. Crimson, moving like a duelist, a smirk that said he was already tasting victory. And Block, slow, steady, unreadable. Fingers curled near his belt, waiting.

Noose smirked. Slow. Certain. "Took your time."

Pip did the math. Six against five. But Darrik and Gull were half-dead already, and Rat-Eye wasn't much of a fighter. Bad odds. For a breath, it looked like they might talk. Pip caught the flicker of calculation in Noose's eyes—measuring, weighing. Was this a fight worth taking, now that Pip and Darrik weren't standing where The Knife had left them?

"You're nothing but Slag drift, Noose," Rat-Eye spat. "Soon to be gone."

Noose's mouth twitched. Almost a smirk. "We'll see."

Then steel rang out, and it was all crashing bodies and chaos. Gull met Hollow's blade first. She was quick. He was desperate. He feinted, twisted, buried his knife in her throat. She gurgled, staggered, but before he could pull free, Choke was on him. The garrote looped fast, cutting deep. Gull convulsed, hands clawing, useless. Rat-Eye lunged, her dagger flashing—once, twice—cutting Choke open. He slumped. Blood pooled.

Darrik clashed with Split. The bigger man fought brutal, hacking wild. Darrik ducked, drove his blade deep, but Split's knife found his ribs at the same time. Both men dropped. Blood soaking the dirt.

Salt fought like a man who knew he wasn't seeing morning. He caught Block's wrist mid-swing, snapped it clean, then slammed his blade up under the ribs. Block choked, blood spilling over Salt's arm. But as Salt yanked his blade free, Noose was already behind him. The knife slid in, straight through the back. Salt jolted; coughed red. Collapsed. Noose twisted the blade slow, deliberate. Drew it free. Watched Salt claw at the ground, then shoved him onto his side. Just to watch the life drain out.

Pip and Crimson circled, fire spitting embers between them. The heat warped the air, twisted the world, turned Crimson into something less than man, more than beast. A shadow moving too smooth, too eager. He grinned. Drew it out. Enjoyed the pause before the cut. Pip didn't move. Stayed low. Coiled. Watched for weakness. Crimson's weight rolled effortless between steps. His blade was loose, lazy. Too easy. Too confident.

Then Crimson moved.

Pip barely saw the strike coming. Crimson moved like a viper, knife flashing in the firelight before sinking between Pip's ribs. A sharp, wet pressure bloomed in his lung. Slow at first. Then the pain hit— white-hot, searing, like molten iron poured straight into his flesh. His breath caught. The world shuddered sideways. Knees buckled. He hit the ground hard, hands pressing to the wound, warmth spilling between his fingers. His pulse pounded thick in his ears. A ragged breath—wet, wrong. Blood flecked his lips.

Crimson's grin cut through the haze. He yanked the blade free. Agony.

The hall groaned. The fire had eaten too much. The weight shifted. Beams cracked, the rafters bowing inward. A deafening snap split the night as the roof collapsed, a thunderous roar of embers and smoke swallowing the room.

Pip swayed, the world narrowing to flickering orange and black. His body sagged, blood seeping into the dirt, pulling something vital with it. Cold crept up his limbs. Distant. Dull. Like the ground was swallowing him whole.

Then—

A whisper. Not sound. Something deeper. Curling through his ribs like smoke.

His fingers twitched.

The Crooked Dagger. Nestled against his heart. Hidden. Calling. His hand rose, slow, fumbling against the leather strap. Thinking was slipping away, lost in the pull of the wound. His fingers closed around the hilt. Small. Twisted. Dark as wet ink. The edges shifted, blurred, like it couldn't decide where the blade began. It drank the firelight. Bent the shadows. Cold—deeper than cold. An absence. A shudder ran through him. His breath hitched, then steadied. The pain dulled. Faded. His limbs stopped shaking. The fog in his mind burned away, sharpening to a clear, unnatural stillness. His heartbeat slowed, then leveled. Steady. Too steady.

He pushed himself up. Deliberate. Measured. Crimson was staring. The knife fighter's grin vanished. His stance shifted, weight rolling uncertain. Blade raised—but not moving forward. Not yet. His eyes flicked to Pip's hand. To the Crooked Dagger.

His mouth parted. "That's not—"

Pip moved. Too fast. Too precise. The Crooked Dagger caught Crimson's wrist—then his throat. No resistance. No struggle. A clean, quiet thing. A breath. A whisper. Crimson shuddered. A wet, choking sound. His legs gave out before his body understood it was dead. He hit the ground. Blood pooling. Mouth half-open, trying to finish something that no longer mattered.

Noose stared. The weight between his feet shifted. His blade lifted an inch—an instinct to fight, a deeper instinct to run. But he hesitated. Pip didn't. Inside his guard. Close enough to hear the first ragged pull of breath as the Crooked Dagger slid under Noose's ribs. A sharp, quiet sound. He stiffened. Gasped.

Pip twisted. Something dark unraveled. A thread pulled. A tether snapped. Noose's body jerked, not like a dying man, but like something had been pulled loose. His mouth opened—silent, stretched, too wide. Then he was gone, his corpse folding in on itself, something missing from within.

The Crooked Dagger pulsed in his grip, like it still wasn't done. Pip stared at his hand — at the fingers wrapped around something that felt alive. The silence pressed in. He didn't breathe. Didn't blink. His limbs ached — but not from the fight. From *something else*. Something pulled. Still pulling. He didn't recognize the hands holding the blade.

Pip stood among the bodies. Firelight flickered against the blade. His fingers curled tight around the hilt. The air pulsed. Blood. Smoke. Something else. Something deep.

He took a breath.

The whisper was gone.

Aieria didn't return to the streets alone. But she didn't retreat, either. She had tasted freedom, and she needed it. It was just a question of how she would get what she wanted.

Indaros. Her living shadow. She needed muscle, and he had plenty. She would carve out her own space in Port Gatos, and for that, she needed a man who answered to her—not to coin, not to fear, but to something deeper. Loyalty, admiration, perhaps even desire. And Indaros, despite himself, would give her all three.

Kael would never approve, so she wouldn't ask. All she needed was for Indaros to become more loyal to her than he was to Kael's gold. And whatever else Kael held over him. Fortunately, she had time. And when she turned her mind to Indaros, he really wasn't that complicated.

Midday meal in the Brass Griffin Inn's common room. Not in her room.

"Indaros. I don't like eating alone. Sit with me."

Begrudging, he obeyed. He must.

At first, he sat stiffly, eating in silence—a reluctant presence rather than a companion. But familiarity dulled resistance. The conversations lengthened; the silences grew companionable. Aieria learned the rhythm of his moods. Meals together became routine, not because he had to, but because somewhere along the way, he had stopped thinking of it as a duty.

She got him talking. First about the weather. Then his favourite food.

She turned to the cook. "Myrell, can we get hakis shank in Gatos?"

A few more days, and she wove it casually into conversation: "You fought for the Sky Kingdom. You must have been trained well."

Indaros barely glanced at her. "Trained to kill. Not the same thing."

Aieria tilted her head, watching him. "And now that training lets you protect me."

He scoffed. "Gets me good coin. That's what matters."

She let the thought hang, then dropped it — planting the seed without pressing.

The next day, she asked, "How would I defend myself?"

"You wouldn't," he answered. "You've Kael's protection. Should be enough."

"Should be?" she asked, holding his eyes for a moment, her expression wounded. He looked away, scowling.

She got him talking about more personal things. His home. His parents. Surprisingly, he had a small collection of ships in bottles. She hadn't taken him for a lover of the sea.

She enjoyed his company. A careless touch — a hand brushing his as she reached for a cup. Her gaze lingered, just long enough to register — too long to forget, too short to name.

By the time Kael next visited, things were different. Under Kael's watchful eye, Indaros was distant and gruff, merely her guard. She played the distant Queen. But they shared an unspoken agreement: Kael must not learn of them.

Then she merely needed to wait for Kael to leave.

She stood by the window of her room, fingers resting lightly on the sill, the glow of the setting sun casting warm streaks across her room. He stood by the door, arms crossed, his stance deliberately neutral. The space between them stretched taut, unspoken things hanging in the air, weighty and unacknowledged. The sun was setting, and the light played along her skin as she engaged him in casual conversation.

Then, "Teach me how to fight."

"You're not made for fighting."

She turned herself to him.

"You said it yourself. This city is not kind. What if I don't have your protection?"

He stared at her. Torn.

She stepped close.

"Tomorrow night. The courtyard."

He had turned away gruffly, but here he was. The night air curled thick with the scent of brine and damp stone, slipping through the half-open courtyard behind the inn. The ground beneath Aieria's bare feet was packed dirt, uneven with loose stones — an unkind surface for a fight, but then, Port Gatos was not a kind place.

"Should break your nose," he muttered, as if speaking to himself. "That's how you teach a noble to fight. Take the arrogance out of them."

Aieria lifted a brow, lips curving ever so slightly. "Do I still seem arrogant to you?"

She wore cotton drawstring trousers and a sleeveless tunic — plain, functional. But the way she moved in them, even bruised and barefoot, still drew the eye. She didn't have to seduce. Just be seen.

Indaros didn't answer. Instead, he tossed her a dagger. She caught it with careful fingers, rolling the hilt in her palm. It was lighter than she expected.

"Why a dagger?" she asked, testing the weight.

"'Cause you're small," he said bluntly. "And soft." His shoulders shifted, loose and at ease, a man entirely within his element. "Which means you don't fight fair."

She had expected as much. Port Gatos had no rules. Only survivors.

"Come on, then," he said, lazy in his stance. "Show me what you think you know."

Aieria didn't hesitate. She moved swiftly, aiming low—a calculated stab to the ribs, clean and efficient. Indaros caught her wrist before the blade got close.

"Too slow."

He twisted. Pain shot up her arm, sharp and immediate. A flick of his weight sent her spinning, off balance—before she could counter, she was flat on her back, the breath driven from her lungs. She coughed, fingers tightening around the dagger. Above her, Indaros stood impassive, the moonlight catching the edge of his gaze.

"That's what happens when you think a blade makes you dangerous," he said. "You move like a court duelist. Think I'll stand still and let you dance?"

Aieria exhaled, rolling to her feet. "Again."

Indaros shrugged. "If you insist."

The next attempt fared no better. Nor the next. Each time, she struck. Each time, he was faster. Sharper. Stronger. And each time, he sent her crashing to the ground. Her breath came harder now, sweat stinging her eyes. Her arms ached from breaking her falls. Her hands throbbed from gripping the dagger too tightly. Indaros watched her, expression unreadable. Her body still waited for wings that weren't there. Her balance remembered flight. Her bones didn't. She wiped her mouth with the back of her hand. She was missing something.

Then she remembered his words — you don't fight fair.

Aieria moved again, but this time she feinted. She lunged high, watched his stance shift — then dropped low, her foot snapping toward his knee. Indaros didn't fall for it. He shifted smoothly, caught her by the shoulder, and in one ruthless motion, sent her sprawling again. The impact jarred her ribs. Her vision flared white. The dagger skittered from her fingers into the dirt. She groaned, rolling onto her back.

Indaros crouched beside her, shaking his head. A flicker of concern passed through his eyes. She placed a hand on his chest. "I'm fine."

"Not bad," he admitted. "But not good enough."

Aieria blinked up at him, breath ragged, frustration burning in her chest. She had never been strong. But she had always been clever. And it hadn't saved her tonight.

Indaros stood, pulling away, offering no hand.

"You're fast, but you don't have the strength yet," he said, already turning.

And then he was gone, leaving her in the dirt, the dagger cold at her side.

She lay still, staring up at the darkened sky. Her body ached. But a smile spread across her lips.

Yet.

She would get stronger. She would learn.

And soon, he wouldn't even remember choosing her.

# Chapter 7.    White Lies and Black Blood

The Butcher's Guildhouse crouched ahead, dark and sagging against the fog-heavy night. Pip's breath rattled, wet and wrong, every step a fresh needle of pain in his ribs. He should be dead. He knew that. But the Crooked Dagger had pulled him back, not with kindness, but with something colder. Crueler. Now the pain was back, sharp and real, proof that he was still breathing. Darrik slumped against him, half-dead, bleeding even before Split's knife found his ribs. They had crawled out of fire and blades, but survival didn't feel like much of a victory. More like the punchline to a bad joke.

Pip's fingers drifted instinctively toward the dagger hidden beneath his coat. Even sheathed, he felt it — cold, hungry, restless. It whispered promises of control, whispers that sounded too much like his own voice. Sometimes he wondered whether it was the dagger pulling him back each time, or if it was something in himself — something darker, something that welcomed the pain as proof he was still here. The Crooked Dagger had saved him, yes, but each survival felt less like victory and more like surrendering another piece of himself

The porch groaned under his boots. The door swung open before he could touch it.

The Knife stood there, lantern light slicing his face

into hard lines. His gaze swept over them—Darrik, then Pip. Still standing. Still bleeding. For a breath, something flickered in his expression. Not relief. Not concern. Just surprise. Then it was gone, smoothed over with a slow smirk.

"Well," The Knife drawled. "Looks like you've had a night."

Pip didn't stop. Just shoved past, dragging Darrik inside. "He needs a sawbones."

The Knife snapped his fingers. One of his men moved fast, hauling Darrik away into the back. Pip flexed his fingers, feeling the weight of the last hour still pressing into his bones. He turned back to The Knife.

"You set us up."

The Knife's brow lifted. The room stretched quiet. "That so?"

Pip's knuckles ached. "White Hall was a grave before we walked in. You knew Rat-Eye would come."

The Knife showed teeth—not in a smile, but the thing that came before one. "You're here, aren't you? Means I was right. Knew you could handle yourselves." He let the words settle, watching Pip like he was turning something over in his head, weighing it.

Then, like it had just occurred to him, The Knife asked, "What happened to Darrik?"

Pip swallowed the pain. "Gull."

The Knife's expression barely shifted, but Pip caught the weight of it. That was enough. Gull was dangerous enough.

Then came the real test. "So. What happened at White Hall?"

Pip met his gaze.

"Rat-Eye came heavy. Darrik didn't want blood, but she was already knee-deep in it. Something set the fire—maybe her, maybe not. The place burned fast. Darrik found a way out. We ran. Her crew followed."

He let it settle. "Noose went down. Gull too. Crimson…"

The blade pulsed on his ribs. Still sheathed, but not silent. Like it remembered the kill. Like it was waiting.

"I slit his throat."

The Knife's gaze sharpened. "And Rat-Eye?"

Pip held the silence a beat. "Slipped the fire. Didn't follow."

The Knife smiled—but only with his mouth. "Pity."

The Knife studied him, weighing the words. Then, slow and deliberate, he nodded. "So that's how it went. Rat-Eye shows up with her whole crew, White Hall burns to the ground, and somehow you and Darrik are the only ones left standing. And no one to say otherwise."

Silence thickened.

The Knife turned to one of his men. "Go to White Hall. Bring me something real."

The man nodded, slipping into the night.

The Knife turned back to Pip. "If you're lying, Pip, I'll know soon enough."

Pip just shrugged, masking the coil of tension in his gut. "Then I guess we'll see."

Later, when the sawbones had taken Darrik and the blood had cooled, Pip sat in the Guildhouse's outer hall, hands empty but still twitching. The dagger whispered nothing. But it didn't need to. He could feel it watching.

**Chapter 8.     A Song for A Fallen Queen**

---

The bruises were expected now. The ache was constant—welts, bruises, the burn of overworked muscles. She no longer flinched—these things no longer unsettled her. Pain was the price of refinement. Of control. Indaros did not coddle. He struck when she faltered, punished mistakes with ruthless efficiency—a twist of the wrist, a sudden hook to the ribs, a well-placed sweep that sent her to the ground. He was stronger. Faster. He fought like a man who had seen death up close and learned to avoid it. And she cursed him for it.

And yet—she improved.

Her stance no longer wavered. Her grip no longer slipped. Her blade moved in precise, deliberate arcs, seeking flesh, exploiting weakness. She was still smaller. Still weaker. But brute strength had never been the only path to power. Pain had taught her something more valuable: how to fight without honour, how to win without mercy.

And Indaros—he had softened. Not in the way he fought her. In that, he remained merciless. But his protests had dulled, shifting from firm resistance to something else—grudging loyalty, perhaps. Or resignation.

Later, in the rancid warmth of a dockside tavern, Aieria watched Indaros nurse a drink like it had betrayed him.

"We shouldn't be out here," Indaros muttered. His voice carried no real conviction. "Something happens, Kael'll have my head."

Aieria took a slow sip of the bitter ale in her hand, unfazed. "Then stay back at the Brass Griffin," she teased.

"And do what? Count ceiling beams?" He scoffed.

Indaros glanced around the dimly lit tavern, the rough-hewn tables sticky with old ale, the air thick with the scent of fish and sweat. Always watching. Always wary. He wrinkled his nose. "This city stinks."

She inhaled, the sharp scent of salt and fish mingling with the acrid bite of pitch and damp wood. Port Gatos was layered, its wealth stacked precariously over its filth, its prosperity propped up by shadows and debts never paid in full. The docks groaned under the weight of trade both legitimate and illicit, a restless artery where merchants haggled over fortunes, thieves plucked purses from fools, and the Wharfdogs watched everything, slipping unseen through the maze of piers and warehouses. Deals were whispered in dark corners, promises made, and bargains broken before dawn. But power did not live here. It was merely trafficked through.

The air stank of tallow smoke and sour ale, heat trapped under the low ceiling like breath held too long. The wooden beams sagged under the weight of years, stained dark with grease and time. Laughter barked from a nearby table, the coarse voices of dockworkers mingling with the occasional clatter of dice on splintered wood. A woman in a threadbare dress wove between the tables, balancing a tray of drinks, her eyes scanning for easy marks.

Through the grime-streaked window beside them, Aieria looked up at the High Ward. The salt in the air triggered old reflex—muscles she no longer had tensed to adjust for balance. Her posture corrected itself by instinct, and for a moment, absence ached sharper than pain. The High Ward. A world apart. Its thick stone walls cut a clean divide between power and everything beneath it, its gates unyielding. Beyond those gates, influence moved quietly—through ledgers, through ink and gold, through whispered agreements where blood rarely had to be spilled. She had once stood in such spaces, smiling and admired, playing in the parry and trust of court intrigue. Even from here, she could see the silhouettes of finely dressed men and women drifting through candlelit parlors, their lives untouched by the filth below. Power did not dwell in places like this tavern—it waited up there, behind locked gates and guarded doors. For now. But not forever.

She let the thought settle, rolling it over in her mind. Strength was necessary, but strength alone would not open those gates. Gold. Influence. Information. If she wanted to carve out her place, she needed all three.

"Tell me about Port Gatos' rulers," she said, letting her gaze drift toward the lanterns glowing above, their soft flicker catching on polished stone and the wrought-iron fences that guarded wealth from the city below. "The ones behind those walls."

He scoffed. "Gatos doesn't have rulers like you Aier. Just money."

"There's a City Watch. There must be courts, rules of trade."

"Courts are bought. Watch takes coin like the rest. Lords? Just a bunch of backstabbing bastards clawing for the top."

She turned and leaned forward, tilting her head just so, letting her voice soften. "But you know their names, don't you?"

Indaros exhaled, the tension in his shoulders slipping. "A few. Everyone does."

Aieria said nothing, simply watching him, letting the silence linger. Silence was a tool; one she had been trained to wield.

"I guess Lord Aedric Kest would be at the top" Indaros muttered, thinking. "Been running the trade routes since forever. Richer than a king. Smarter too, I figure. He's not the sort for lavish parties and all that. But I bet he could buy half the city if he wanted.

"Then there's Lord Branneth Yerris. He's got the shipyards. No boat hits water 'less he gets a cut. Old now, but still holds the docks tight. Half the captains hate him, half swear by him.

"And there's Lady Evandra Tressan. Deals in luxuries—spices, gems, Aier silks. I don't know. Stuff nobles love. She's got hands in everything soft and expensive, and she doesn't mind people knowing it. She runs those high-class brothels in the High Ward, where silk and secrecy are worth more than gold." Indaros hesitated, rubbing the back of his neck, suddenly realizing the kind of trade he was discussing with her. Aieria caught the shift and let out a soft laugh.

Indaros cleared his throat, glancing away, suddenly interested in the grain of the table. Then, with a forced casualness, he pressed on, "You want to talk lavish, Tressan's the one. Apparently, she hosts a party for the super-rich each year on the Night of Lanterns—all the nobles climb over each other to get invited."

"And, of course, there's Solivar…"

Aieria's grip tightened around her cup. The name echoed in her memory, distant but unmistakable.

"Shann Solivar. Gatos' famous bard. Surely you heard of him? He plays in the grandest halls, drinks with the richest merchants, and still finds his way into the grimiest taverns just to keep the common folk singing his name. Nobles praise his wit, sailors swear by his luck, and every girl in the High Ward claims he's whispered a song just for her. Ain't got Kest's wealth or Yerris' reach, but he don't need it. He's not a Lord—but he might as well be. Every merchant's daughter—hell, every lord's daughter—got a story about him."

Yes. Aieria had danced with Solivar once, beneath chandeliers dripping with crystal and gold. In Velirion, a lower Sky City, one of the few places where human wealth might buy an invitation into Aier halls. It had been rare enough to see a human at such an event, rarer still to see one who carried himself as if he belonged. He had bowed over her hand with a smile meant to disarm, his beauty almost unnatural for a man of his kind. His words had been effortless, his charm polished. He had flirted, subtly, but deliberately.

She had seen only his species, not his ambition. Back then, she had been a princess, untouchable, too far above him to care. She had smiled, been gracious, played the role expected of her—but she had dismissed him. As all Aier dismissed humans.

She would not dismiss him now. Solivar could be a bridge—one she would have to cross carefully. He moved through circles she could not yet enter, held influence she might, in time, learn to navigate. If she played it well, she could gain more than just access. She could learn how power in Gatos truly worked.

She set her drink down, decisions already solidifying. "I need to see him."

Indaros blinked, then sighed, rubbing his temple. "Of course you do."

Aieria smiled, tilting her head slightly. "Don't you want a keepsake? Maybe a lock of his famous hair?"

He groaned. "Kael's gonna kill me."

Kael wasn't here. He hadn't been for months. She no longer missed his silence, or wondered why. Whatever claim he thought he had on her had withered in his absence. He clearly had no use for her. Perhaps he never did. But she didn't need to understand Kael's calculations and subterfuges. She'd no longer be bound by him, or anyone. Kael thought she would sit passively by while he pulled her strings. That was his error. Let him stay absent, spinning his webs. She could spin webs of her own.

# Chapter 9.    Butchering the Butchers

Darrik had crawled out of White Hall half-dead, blood pooling inside him where it shouldn't have been. He remembered the fire, the smoke, the crack of beams collapsing. The knife in his ribs. Pip dragging him out. He hadn't thanked him. He couldn't. There was no space left in him for gratitude — only pain.

Then came the bed. Weeks of it. A month of sweating through ragged fever, burning up while the gang bled itself out. Every day he woke up to a world that had shrunk around him. Smaller. Meaner. More broken. He was alive, sure — but nothing about it felt like winning. Every time he woke, the world had changed just a little more.

The first time he stood on his own, he realized the Butchers had kept dying while he was too sick to stop it. They were ghosts now. Thin and hollow. Just a name people still spat out of habit.

It started quiet. A few missing men. Then a few more. The right people turning up dead in the wrong places. The Butchers joked at first. Bad luck. Cost of doing business.

Then the bodies kept showing up. And they weren't just bodies. They were warnings.

Leech disappeared first. The Knife wanted to see for

himself. Brothel basement. Stink of blood and rot. Someone had gone to work on him with his own tools, stripped him like a carcass. The Butcher, butchered.

Then Bloodpact. Found where he always sat, drink untouched, head slumped forward. No struggle. Just a sigil burned into the table. No one sat there again.

The laughter stopped. Fear crawled in. The ones still breathing started watching their backs, jumping at shadows. Confidence rotted just as fast as the corpses.

The Knife didn't wait. Couldn't. He hit back. Fast. Low Tide turned up in the harbour, throat open, bobbing in red water. Drift went next, arms snapped, skull caved in, left in an alley near the shipyard. But for every hit, Rat-Eye had one waiting. Every move The Knife made fell apart before it could take root.

The war spread. Spilled into every alley. Stained every street. The Knife got paranoid. Too many ghosts in the dark. Men got themselves gutted for showing up late, cut just for hesitating.

But that wasn't half their trouble.

Pip had always been dangerous, sharp-edged in a way that kept people at arm's length. Darrik had never minded that. Pip was useful. A blade in the dark. But since White Hall, there was something else. Something harder to name.

Pip stuck to him. Sat by him each night. Almost like a shadow, he was just attached to Darrik. Watching. Taking something in. But what? Darrik wasn't sure. Pip had dragged him out of White Hall, kept him breathing when the fever might have taken him, but there was no comfort in his presence. Sometimes, in his fever, it felt like Pip was just curiously watching him die.

Darrik wasn't afraid of him. Pip wasn't a threat to him. But that didn't mean he liked what he was seeing. Pip was too still when he stood, too quiet when he moved. And sometimes, when Darrik caught him in the corner of his eye, it was like Pip wasn't even breathing. Just there, waiting.

Darrik thought about that night, about the fire, the smoke, the way Pip had pulled him out of the wreckage. He thought he'd seen something—something he couldn't explain. Pip had gone down, should've stayed down, but then he was moving, cutting through the dark like a blade in the gut. And Noose—Noose hadn't just died. Darrik had seen men die before. This was different. Noose had folded in on himself, like something had been pulled out of him, something vital.

He didn't believe in curses, ghosts, or anything else the Slag whispered about in dark corners. But some nights, when the light hit Pip just wrong, when the air turned heavy, a thought crawled in like rot beneath the skin—maybe White Hall had taken something out of Pip. Or maybe it had put something else back in. But he never said a word.

The fever finally broke. Darrik knew he was going to live, but his body hadn't caught up to the idea yet. Everything ached. The world moved faster than he could follow.

Rat-Eye's war on the Butchers wasn't getting any better. The Butchers were falling apart one knife at a time, and all he could do was watch it happen. Try not to fall again. Try not to need saving.

He'd come back from the edge. For what, though? To limp behind a dying gang, to watch one man after another slit their own throat in slow motion? The Butchers were sliding toward the gutter, and no one was steering. There was no one left to pull them back—and if there was, no one would listen anyway.

One night, down in the Slag's dockside alleys, two gangs crossed paths. Butchers and Wharfdogs. Fists landed. Blades bit. When it ended, two bodies lay in the gutter, blood pooling between the stones. Two more groaned in the dirt, too broken to rise.

Business wasn't business anymore. Trade routes sat empty. Debts went unpaid. The Guildhouse wasn't a place for deals—it was a bunker. Guards at every door. Eyes never still. Hands never far from steel. Nobody moved alone. Even with backup, trust ran thin. Every errand, every whisper, carried weight. No one worried about coin anymore. Only about seeing the next morning.

Some ran. Thought distance might save them. Sometimes it did. Sometimes it didn't. Dust vanished. No blood. No struggle. Just drag marks in the mud leading to dark water. Drowned, maybe. Or maybe something waited out there. Patient. The Widow thought herself safe in the High Ward — until someone proved her wrong. No struggle. Just her body on the floor, candles low, eyes wide, staring at nothing.

Then the Wharfdog's Serpent called out the Butcher's Knuckles for a bare-knuckle fight in the Low Ward. Neutral ground. A death match.

Knuckles laughed. The man lived for breaking people open.

Darrik was barely two days back on his feet when The Knife called him up. "Knuckles needs to make it through the fight tonight." Clipped words. Businesslike.

Darrik nodded.

The plan was simple: get Knuckles to the fight, watch him win, and bring him back breathing. Darrik wasn't in any condition to fight. His ribs still ached, his muscles weak from weeks in bed, but he could stand. That was enough. Knuckles could handle himself in the ring — Darrik just had to make sure the fight stayed clean, and that no one tried to settle a grudge on the way out. If anyone got serious, Pip would handle it. Darrik didn't need to tell him. Pip already knew. He had that look about him, like a blade waiting to be drawn, like he was hoping someone would try something. If he gave people the creeps, all the better.

Simple. At least, it should've been.

And yet, Knuckles still ended up dead, choking on treachery. He should've won. But the first punch was slow. Weak. His strength gave out. His breath choked in his throat. His knees buckled. He collapsed to the dirt, the laughter turning cruel. By the time Darrik stepped in, stopped the fight, Knuckles was already gone. Just like that. All that muscle, all that pride—crumpled like he'd never mattered. The Butchers had lost more than a man that night. They'd lost face. Wherever she was, Rat-Eye was gloating. Taking the Butchers apart.

The Butchers still held the Slag, but it wasn't theirs anymore—not really. The swagger, the cruelty, the easy grins—thinned like smoke after rain. Voices dropped lower. Men moved in groups, even when they didn't need to. The Knife still gave orders, still sat at the head of the guild hall, but he looked smaller now. Worn. Like the paranoia was eating him from the inside. Rat-Eye's men still prowled. Still struck when it suited them. Always just out of reach.

And while the rest of them were on a knife's edge, waiting for the next strike, Pip came and went as it pleased him. No one stopped him. No one even tried. And when men turned up dead—ones who should've been too well-guarded, too careful—Pip was never there. Always somewhere else. Always absent, but never far.

Darrik saw it in The Knife's eyes. He suspected. Maybe even knew. Maybe Pip was in on it. Darrik couldn't tell. But The Knife never called Pip out, never questioned him. The Knife had never liked Pip. He'd kept him close, because men like Pip were useful, but there'd never been trust. Pip was too quiet, too quick, too much like something that didn't belong in the world but refused to leave it. Now, though, it was worse. The Knife wasn't just wary— he was careful. A man who wasn't afraid of anything was watching where he stepped. Avoiding Pip's path. Not looking at him too long, as if it were bad luck, as if something would take notice if he did.

And the men noticed. They saw who the real predator in the room was. Pip had never been one of them. But now, even the Butchers acted like he was something else entirely. It wasn't good. Not for the Butchers. Not for The Knife. There couldn't be two monsters at the top. And yet, there Pip was. Not fighting for it. Not reaching for it. Just there, waiting. Like a shadow that wasn't sure if it should move— or swallow the whole room instead.

The Butchers were still standing. But the blood was already leaking through the floorboards—and no one dared to look down.

# Chapter 10.    Feathers and Intrigue

Solivar stormed into his apartment, slamming the door behind him with enough force to set the crystal panes quivering. The city outside hummed, distant voices rising in a symphony of revelry, laughter and song spilling from the High Ward's taverns like wine from an overfilled cup. Beneath it all, the rhythmic clatter of carriage wheels on uneven stone whispered the night's continuation. Gatos would celebrate until dawn, unconcerned with the particular ruin of one man's evening.

A streak of red stained his cuff—wine, or was it blood? No, wine. The indignity of the stain stung worse than the insult itself. His collar hung askew, his cravat had been abandoned to some forgotten fate, and the sour tang of humiliation lingered on his tongue like an old lover overstaying her welcome.

He shed his boots with a careless kick, one striking the leg of his writing desk and sending a half-finished scroll fluttering to the floor. "Bloody fools," he muttered, dragging a hand through his graying curls, fingers tangling in the evidence of his years. "Wretched hag." His voice was hoarse, laced with the remnants of wine and fury, his thoughts blurred by both. The candlelight above flickered, shadows bleeding across the ceiling like ink spilled upon parchment.

He had grown old. Not in body—no, the mirror still reflected a man who had danced with queens, whose voice had once commanded the breathless silence of courts—but in relevance. The nobles still hummed *The Ballad of the Falling Star*, still sighed wistfully at *The Lover's Dirge*, still demanded *The Last Dance at Aetherion*. But those belonged to another Solivar, one who had yet to be reduced to an artifact, dusted off when the mood struck, then set aside once more.

The night had begun with promise—Lord Dervain's estate, a fine table, an audience of Gatos' most affluent parasites eager for his wit. And yet, like a poorly penned play, the second act had collapsed under its own weight. Lady Aliseth—the once-devoted patron of his every verse—had dismissed him with a flick of her fan, turning her attention to a younger, fresher performer. Solivar, ever the fool, had pressed too far, his wit turning barbed. And for his trouble, a glass of red wine dashed into his face, to the delighted gasps of the assembled vultures.

Then, the final insult—escorted out like some drunken wretch, his exit not a grand departure, but a quiet shuffling away from their laughter.

The nobles wanted only two things—either a sycophantic paean to their imagined grandeur or a tired recitation of an old favourite. They craved echoes, not art. And Solivar, for all his patience, was growing weary of playing minstrel to their vanity.

Kings bled and rotted, but words endured. They

dictated who sat at the table, who was remembered, who was cast in gold and who was swept into the quiet grave of history. Yet tonight, he had been made to feel like a relic, an actor overstaying his welcome on a stage that no longer wished to hold him.

He reached for the decanter, the one mercy of the evening yet unspoiled, when a knock interrupted the quiet.

Soft. Quick.

He stilled; glass poised mid-pour.

No servant knocked like that.

For the briefest moment, he entertained a most idiotic notion—that Lady Aliseth had come to him after all, slipping past the ever-watchful eyes of the High Ward, drawn back by regret, by longing. That her laughter at his expense had been nothing more than a cruel overture, and this—this—was her grand finale. A breathless confession in the candlelight, a whispered assurance that none of it had mattered.

The fantasy barely had time to bloom before disgust pruned it at the stem. Gods, was he truly that desperate? That ridiculous? A sneer curled at the edge of his lips, more at himself than the imagined folly. He exhaled sharply, shaking off the indulgence, jaw tightening against the bitter taste of his own self-pity. Aliseth would never come. The world had no habit of granting second acts to men already ushered off the stage.

Solivar rose, stockinged feet whispering against the silk-woven rug, the fabric cool against his skin. The city beyond his windows hummed—a chorus of distant revelry, rolling waves, and the occasional drunken oath carried on the salt-laced air. His fingers undid the latch without hesitation. Hesitation was for men who feared danger. Solivar only feared irrelevance. He cracked the door.

Nothing.

Only the cool breath of the evening air, the scent of brine drifting in from the bay.

And at his feet, an envelope.

He knelt, fingers brushing the parchment. Unmarked—no crest, no flourish, only the faintest smudge of wax where a hand had pressed it shut. Yet there was weight to it, something deliberate in its placement, something that made the air shift subtly around it. Not an ordinary letter. A declaration, a game piece set upon the board.

He stepped back inside, relatching the door with a quiet click. The chamber around him was a study in calculated decadence—Tahl'Varethian mahogany shelves sagging under the weight of books stacked without care, scrolls unspooled over low tables, goblets of spiced wine half-drunk and long abandoned. The air was thick with the perfume of old parchment, candle wax, and the lingering ghosts of lovers who had come and gone, leaving only their scent woven into the velvet-draped settee.

The flame in the lantern shivered, casting jagged strokes of light across the walls — shadows that took shape, familiar specters from the archives of his past. Aedrin Velcor, the poet who once challenged him in verse and left the city in disgrace. Orvin Cassel, the merchant who had dared to withhold a debt and found his business crumbling in the wake of an unfortunate rumour. And, of course, Lady Aliseth, her laughter still clinging like the last sting of wine against his skin.

Solivar slid a knife from his belt — ornate, a gift from a lord whose name he had already half-forgotten — and sliced through the wax.

Inside, a single slip of parchment.

No introduction. No signature. Just a few carefully chosen lines.

———

*You've told the story of Aier, but not the truth.*

*You've sung of a fallen Queen, but not the dance she shared before the fire.*

*Would you like to know how it ends?*

———

Solivar went still. The words coiled around him,

weightless yet inescapable, slipping beneath his skin, threading through his ribs like a whisper too close, too knowing. They pressed against old bones, stirring older ghosts.

The dance.

He had danced with many, whispered promises against candlelit skin, laughed in the arms of nobility and thieves alike. But some moments did not dull with time. Some things refused to fade. And she—she—had never faded. And if someone remembered—truly remembered—then maybe he hadn't faded either.

Aieria.

The name settled on his tongue like the memory of a half-finished verse, rich with echoes of warmth and firelight, of silk-pressed skin and whispered defiance. A note unresolved, yet never forgotten.

His fingers tightened around the parchment, knuckles white against the edges. No name. No demand. Just an invitation, wrapped in silence. Beside it, something delicate. Something gilded. A feather. Gilded, delicate. Impossible. He knew it. Knew what it meant. What it shouldn't mean. Yet there it was—unburned, unburied, and daring him to remember. Solivar turned it over, watching the firelight dance along its barbs. His lips curled—not in reverence, not in awe, but in something far sharper. Intrigue.

A trick, perhaps. A game. But a lovely one, if it was.

The candlelight flickered, catching in the silver filigree of his writing desk, reflecting off the brass inlay of the mirror that stood slightly cracked in the corner. The city still hummed beyond the terrace doors, drapes swaying in the night breeze, as if beckoning. And for the first time in too long, he felt the slow, curling spark of anticipation—the rare, intoxicating pleasure of a mystery unfolding just for him.

A challenge worthy of him.

He exhaled, a slow, measured breath, letting the silence unfurl before him. He traced the feather's edge, letting the moment settle, letting the words shape themselves into something inevitable. Then, with a soft chuckle, he let the words escape.

"Well," he murmured to the empty room. "This is interesting. And I do love a good ending."

# Chapter 11.    An Alliance in Ink

Salt and lantern smoke drifted on the wind as Aieria climbed. The stone was slick, each foothold deliberate. This wasn't the panic of a cornered girl—it was a skill honed by nights spent in the veins of Gatos. The first time had been clumsy, hesitant, the memory of her fall—of hands grasping, of everything stolen—still fresh in her bones. But she had learned. She had forced her body to adapt, to take to stone and ledges as easily as she had once taken to the skies. There was no hesitation now.

Below, Port Gatos sprawled, its streets winding like veins, the heartbeat of a city that never truly slept. But she had no interest in the city tonight—only in the man who slept above it, high in his private rooms, far removed from the filth and hunger below.

Solivar.

Not far from the High Ward's walls, Indaros waited. He had not liked this plan, had grumbled about the risk, about Kael, about the sheer stupidity of climbing into a man's home when there were safer ways to arrange a meeting. But he had come anyway. Because he always did. He was there as a shadow, unseen but close enough to intervene should things go wrong. If she did not return by dawn, he would come for her. He would not ask permission.

The balcony was dark, its door latched but not

bolted. The bard had grown careless. Or perhaps he believed himself untouchable. A foolish thought in a place like this. Aieria braced against the ledge, testing its strength, then swung herself over with the ease of someone who had learned to be quick, quiet, and unseen.

She straightened, adjusting the mask that covered the lower half of her face. A simple thing—dark cloth, unremarkable—but it served its purpose. Her cloak draped over her shoulders, concealing the careful wrappings across her back, the false weight beneath the fabric. If he looked closely, if he squinted through the candlelight, he might wonder if wings lay hidden beneath. Or perhaps he would think them an elaborate deception. Let him wonder.

Inside, the room flickered with the dying glow of a single candle, its flame guttering in the draft. Solivar was there, sprawled in a chair, one boot kicked off, his vest undone, a half-empty goblet of something rich and dark resting in his palm. He wasn't asleep, but neither was he fully awake. His fingers tapped against the goblet's rim, slow, thoughtful, the mark of a man unraveling his own thoughts.

Aieria stepped forward, letting the wood creak beneath her weight.

Solivar tensed, his hand shifting toward the dagger at his belt, but she lifted a single finger, pressing it against her lips.

His mouth quirked, amusement flickering through the tired lines of his face. But beneath that amusement, curiosity stirred. He studied her, his gaze lingering on the mask, on the drape of her cloak.

"Dramatic. A touch theatrical, even. Should I be honoured or concerned?"

"If I wished to kill you," she murmured, stepping into the light, "you wouldn't have woken up at all."

He sighed, leaning back into his chair, though his sharp eyes remained fixed on her. Amusement curled at the corner of his lips, but behind it, calculation stirred—he was enjoying the game, but he was also trying to see the edges of it, to find the shape of what she wanted.

"You knew I'd come," she said.

Solivar exhaled, swirling the liquid in his goblet. "I suspected." He gestured to his desk, where a folded scrap of parchment lay atop a pile of unfinished verses. Her last note. He had smoothed the creases, but the edges were still soft from being handled. "Your words are lovely, by the way. The first one was clever. The second—impertinent. The third?" He tilted his head, his eyes gleaming with something unreadable. "That one was a challenge."

Aieria smiled beneath the mask. "And you do love a challenge."

His laugh was quiet, but his fingers drummed

against the goblet's rim. "I do. But flattery and riddles only get one so far. Tell me, shadow-climber, why are you really here?"

She tilted her head, allowing a pause long enough to let him wonder. Let him think of the whispers, of the fallen queen who had vanished, of the woman who had once danced in halls of firelite and gold. She saw it flicker across his face—the thought, the question. He did not ask. He was too careful for that. But the seed was planted.

Aieria took her time, moving to his desk, trailing her fingers over the worn edges of parchment, the scattered notes. Words meant to outlive him. That was what he wanted, wasn't it? Not coin, not power—immortality through verse. A name that would never fade.

"I need you to write a ballad."

Solivar tilted his head. "I write many."

"I need this one to matter. To shake the bones of the city." She turned to him, watching for his reaction. "A song that will live forever. A song that will give them something to believe in."

Solivar's gaze sharpened. "Them."

"The people."

He studied her, his fingers drumming against the arm of his chair. "You do understand that inspiration and rebellion walk a fine line?"

"I'm counting on it."

His laugh was soft, but there was steel beneath it. "And where exactly shall this ballad place you? Not in Gatos, surely."

Aieria smiled, slow and knowing. "Let them sing of me in distant lands, in cities untouched by the filth of this one. Let them whisper my name as though I am something long lost, something worth mourning."

His gaze flickered again to her cloak, to the unseen weight it concealed. She felt the hesitation, the silent war between reason and suspicion playing across his face. But she could see it in his eyes, the half-formed question he did not voice. Did he believe? Did he want to believe? She let the silence stretch, let the shadows and candlelight deepen the uncertainty. Mystery was a far sharper blade than truth.

"A martyr in exile?"

"If that's what it takes."

Solivar regarded her for a long moment. Then, with a lazy motion, he poured himself another drink. "A song like that will make you unforgettable."

"Exactly."

She let the weight of her words settle before stepping

closer, resting one hand on the arm of his chair, the other braced against the desk. Close enough that he could see the calculation in her eyes, close enough that he could feel the gravity of what she was asking.

"But that isn't the real plan."

Solivar stilled.

Aieria leaned in, just enough to let the space between them turn into something charged, something deliberate.

"I need more than a song, Solivar. I need a partner."

His brow lifted, skepticism shadowing his expression. "And what exactly do you think I can offer beyond a clever turn of phrase?"

She let a beat pass. Then another.

"You know things."

His fingers tightened around his goblet.

"You know names. Weaknesses. Who they love. Who they owe." She tilted her head. "You have spent years entertaining the high and mighty, weaving their stories into verse. But what if, for once, you stopped writing about them and started using them?"

Solivar arched a brow, his eyes gleamed with something — interest, maybe. Or danger.

"You need a front man," he murmured, his voice quieter now. "Someone to move in the spaces you can't."

Aieria nodded. "And I couldn't find better."

He watched her, weighing the risk, the thrill, the sheer recklessness of it. Then he raised his goblet in a silent toast and drained it dry.

"You do realize," he said slowly, "that stories don't just inspire revolutions. They also get people killed."

Aieria didn't blink. "Only the ones worth remembering."

"Well, then," he said, setting it aside. "Then let's give them something to sing about."

# Chapter 12.    The Lady Iseth Val'Asara

The estate of Edric Kest shimmered, drenched with light and indulgence, a gilded island adrift in the dark sea of Port Gatos, where shadows swam thick with secrets and the scent of ambition clung to the air like perfume. Lanterns swung from golden chains, casting wavering halos over marble terraces. Silk banners of crimson and gold, woven at great cost, billowed from balconies and archways, murmuring their opulence to the wind like courtiers scheming in hushed tones. Perfumed smoke coiled in the halls, thick with the scent of distant spices and the intoxicating warmth of indulgence, each breath a whispered invitation to indulgence. Within, the city's elite drank deep, laughed loudly, and gossiped with the sharp tongues of those who had never known hunger.

At the heart of it all stood Solivar, the evening's golden god, his voice weaving through the crowd like a spell. His latest ballad—*Where Doth Aieria Roam?*—had taken Gatos by storm. It was a song that left listeners leaning forward, a question that refused to be silenced. And now, as he bowed before his enthralled audience, Edric Kest himself—once weighed down by debts and disgrace—hummed the melody under his breath as he strode onto his private balcony, reveling in the heady scent of emberleaf curling through the air. Silk and gemstone adorned his broad frame, his wealth draped across him as conspicuously as the gold that gleamed on his fingers. Not long ago, he had teetered on the edge of ruin, but fortune had smiled upon him. His debts, vanished. His disgrace, erased. And now? Now, he was restored.

The night was warm, the air thick with flowering vines. Beyond the estate walls, Gatos pulsed with its usual schemes and vices, but here, above it all, Edric savoured the knowledge that he had survived. He tapped his fingers against the stone railing, keeping time with Solivar's refrain.

"My lord Kest."

Edric turned, half-drifting in his haze of indulgence as Solivar stepped onto the balcony, a goblet of his own in hand. The bard moved like a man who belonged everywhere and owed fealty to no one. Above them, the heavens sprawled, awash in cobalt and violet, the last vestiges of twilight drowning in the abyss of night. Two moons kept their silent vigil—Anhar, a sliver of silver sharp as a dagger's edge, and Zarim, a watchful giant, its face veiled in restless clouds, as though hoarding secrets it dared not share. Azhra, the red moon of reckoning, was absent tonight. The gods were not watching. The night was lawless.

"A fine evening, is it not? And a finer host," Solivar mused.

Edric chuckled, lifting his goblet. "Flattery is the

breath of bards."

"Ah, but I speak only truths. And I bring a guest to honour such a generous patron." Solivar gestured to the archway behind him. "Might I introduce Lady Iseth Val'Asara, Jewel of Tahl'Vareth?"

Edric's gaze followed as a woman emerged, veiled and radiant, her gown a cascade of silk that clung like shadows. A sheer, embroidered cape draped from her shoulders, moving with an effortless grace that suggested old wealth and deeper secrets. A trace of spice and myrrh lingered in the air around her, mingling with the whisper of silk. She carried herself with the certainty of royalty, though whether that royalty still wore a crown or had long since traded it for cunning was a question left unspoken. Her eyes, pale as morning's first breath, carried the weight of distant horizons, the hush before the dawn when the world holds its breath and waits for fate to stir.

Edric straightened, smoothing the front of his vest, summoning a smile. "A pleasure, my lady."

"The pleasure is mine," she purred, each syllable flowing like silk, her Tahl'Varethian accent measured and deliberate. "I had hoped to find you in such fine spirits."

Solivar leaned against the railing, the picture of a man watching a well-crafted play unfold. "My lord Kest, you are in the presence of one who knows the finer things in life," he mused. "Much like yourself, she has an appreciation for history, for beauty… and for opportunity."

Kest chuckled, swirling his wine. "How could I not? Solivar's song has reminded us all of something greater than ourselves. An exiled queen, lost and waiting, hidden among us. Imagine it!" He laughed lightly. "Why, if she truly lived, I would swear my very estate to her cause. Anything for the Sky Crown."

Iseth tilted her head. "And if she lived, my lord? Would you recognize her?"

Kest hesitated, then laughed again, shaking his head. "Perhaps! But the past is the past, and the future belongs to those who seize it."

"Men like you," she said, stepping closer. The silk of her gown whispered against the stone. "Tell me, my lord, do you still indulge in your favourite escape?"

Kest's smile turned indulgent, the look of a man who had never learned to refuse himself anything. "You know of my vices, then?"

Iseth lifted a hand, a small vial glinting between her fingers. The liquid inside shimmered like moonlight on water, a rare indulgence from the southern isles. She pressed it into his palm with deliberate grace. "A gift," she murmured. "For a man of fine taste."

His fingers curled around the vial; eyes gleaming with anticipation. "You truly are a vision of generosity, my lady."

Solivar laughed. "Come now, Edric. We can't deny a gift from a lady of Tahl'Vareth!"

By the end of the evening, Edric Kest felt the world shifting beneath him, though he barely grasped how or when he had let it happen. Somewhere between Iseth's silk-soft voice and Solivar's easy laughter, his will had been wrapped in velvet and gently guided toward the inevitable. He did not think to resist, nor did he care to. The thought that he had gained something—favour, purpose, a higher calling—settled in his mind like a warm ember, though it was not he who had claimed a prize this night.

Drifting between lucidity and euphoria, his mind swayed like a ship caught between tides. He hung onto their every word, eyes wide with devotion as Iseth leaned close, her whisper a velvet caress against his ear.

"I know the truth, Lord Kest," she breathed. "I know where Aieria hides."

His breath caught. His grip tightened. "Where?"

"Tahl'Vareth." She let the name settle between them like a sacred thing. "Far from the reach of her enemies, waiting. But she does not wait idly. She has allies, loyalists, partners." She traced a single finger down his wrist, letting the implication sink deep. "Do you know why your debts vanished, my lord?"

Kest hesitated, the haze of indulgence swallowing doubt whole. His lips parted, but no words came.

Solivar smirked, sipping his wine. "Because she wished it so."

Edric exhaled slowly, his fingers tightening around the goblet as if he could anchor himself to the present, though the tides of the night had long since pulled him beyond his depth. He blinked, then laughed softly. "She *is* alive," he murmured, nodding to himself, to them, to the night. "The Queen is alive."

Iseth lifted his chin with a single, gentle touch. "She is looking for a partner," she murmured. "A man of means. A man of loyalty."

Kest exhaled sharply, eyes glistening. "Anything that is mine is at the Queen's disposal."

Solivar and Iseth exchanged a glance. Edric, lost in the haze of indulgence and revelation, swirled the last of his wine and exhaled, feeling as though he had just placed a bet on the winning hand, though the game had been played long before he sat at the table.

# Chapter 13.    The Counting House

The Butchers' Guildhouse smelled like blood and dust. Not fresh blood. The kind that settled in, thick and permanent, soaked into floorboards and the cracks between stones. The kind that never left, even after the bodies did.

Pip sat on an old cask, arms loose over his knees, listening to the silence that had set in after the last few months of slaughter. The Butchers weren't what they had been.

The Knife sat at the head of the long, pitted table, looking smaller than he should. His face was leaner, shadows carved under his eyes, the weight of too many betrayals pressing into his shoulders. The war with Rat-Eye had bled him out slow. He wasn't dead yet, but he was getting there.

And Darrik, standing just behind The Knife's chair.

He had a name now. Stone.

The Knife had given it to him the day the summons came from Sargo. The war had run the guild dry, and the Guildmaster had finally weighed in: the fight was over. The Quartermasters had been called together to hear it straight. Darrik's promotion had more to do with necessity than any real desire to make him second. Rat-Eye had cut out all the ones The Knife would've turned to. He needed someone at his side, and Darrik was what was left.

And to his credit, Darrik fit the role. Didn't reach for power like the others had, didn't throw his weight around to make himself seem bigger. Didn't have to. He listened more than he talked, and when he did speak, people shut up to hear it. It wasn't ambition that made him a leader — it was the simple fact that he knew the streets, knew the men, and never pretended to be anything more than what he was.

The door swung open hard enough to rattle the lanterns on the walls.

Chally Finn strode in, practically vibrating, all thin shoulders and too much excitement. "Got one," he declared, hands spread wide, waiting for someone to give a damn.

Nobody moved. The silence stretched, thick and heavy. Pip stayed where he was, watching Finn from the cask, waiting. The flicker of his grin, the way his stance shifted under the weight of the quiet. The first hints of uncertainty, crawling in slow.

Finn hesitated. Then plowed forward anyway. "Near the brickyard by the docks. Rat-Eye's man, walking near the tannery. Thought I'd take the chance. Quick work, clean. No one saw."

The Knife didn't react. Just stared.

Darrik let out a slow breath, jaw working. Pip caught the problem before anyone said a word. From the look on Darrik's face, so did he.

"Gelt & Harvery's tannery?"

Finn nodded, still grinning, like he hadn't realized he was already dead.

Darrik let the silence stretch just long enough for it to sink in. "That's not the docks. Gelt & Harvery's in the Low Ward."

Finn's smile withered.

Darrik didn't blink. "Did you kill him?"

Finn nodded. Not smiling now. "I mean, I think so…"

Darrik tipped his chin at Pip. "Go check it."

Pip shoved off the cask, heading for the door. Behind him, Darrik's voice was ice. "Who was it?"

"I don't know. Some bruiser — big bastard, gold tooth —" Finn's voice wavered, just a little. He glanced around like he expected someone to back him up. No one did. His hands curled slightly. The last of his confidence cracking under the weight of the room.

Pip stopped. Turned.

Darrik ran a hand down his face. "You've got to be rusting me." A sigh. Then, quiet, flat: "You killed Blacktooth's cousin."

Finn blinked. "No—he was Rat-Eye's, he—"

"Only one big bastard with a gold tooth that I know of," Darrik took a step forward, slow, deliberate, "is Korvan Durnvale." Another sigh. "Kid, you just slit the throat of one of Blacktooth's blood. In his own quarter."

Finn's mouth opened, but nothing came out. Fear creeping in behind his eyes.

The Knife finally spoke, voice dull and heavy as an axe coming down. "You better pray he was Rat-Eye's, boy. Otherwise, Blacktooth's coming. And he'll be bringing hell with him."

Pip didn't wait to hear the rest. He was already halfway out the door, heading toward the tannery. Already knowing what he'd find.

---

The Butchers' Guildhouse was quiet. The kind of quiet that squeezed the air tight.

Finn sat stiff in a chair, sweat beading at his temples. He was thinking about running—Pip could see it in the way his hands clenched, in the way his eyes twitched to the door. But there was nowhere to go. Nowhere The Knife would let him go. Letting him slip meant death, not just for him but for The Knife, for whatever was left of the Butchers.

Across from him, The Knife sat with his fingers

tented, face carved from stone. Darrik stood at his shoulder; arms folded. Pip stayed where he always did—just beyond the light, watching.

The knock came sharp. Not a question. A statement. They all knew what it meant before the door even opened.

The messenger stepped inside—wiry, ink-stained fingers, not a fighter, but a man who'd seen enough blood to know his place. He didn't bow, didn't ask permission. Just spoke. "Blacktooth wants a meet. Tonight." His gaze flicked to Finn. "Bring the boy."

Finn flinched like he'd been struck. His breath hitched. No one spoke.

The Knife leaned back, fingers drumming against the armrest. "And?"

The messenger hesitated, just a beat too long. "Said he'd prefer you come ready to settle accounts."

The Knife exhaled slow. That was the answer he'd been waiting for. His mouth pressed into a thin line; his eyes dark. Pip saw the math running behind them. This wasn't just about Finn. Blacktooth wasn't stupid. He knew the Butchers were bleeding out, knew The Knife didn't have the bodies to throw around anymore. This wasn't just a message. It was a demand. And Blacktooth might be asking for a whole lot more than just one dead idiot.

The Knife pushed to his feet. "Tell Blacktooth I'll be

there." His gaze swept the room. "And tell him I'll be bringing what's owed."

The messenger nodded once, then slipped out the door, vanishing into the night.

The Knife turned to Darrik. "We're not walking in light. Blacktooth's going to want more than Finn. We make sure he knows he can't just take whatever he wants."

Darrik's nod was sharp. "How many?"

"All of them." The Knife's jaw tightened. "What's left."

Finn shrank at those words. That was when it hit him—this wasn't just his mistake anymore. It was bigger. And when men like Blacktooth called a meeting, survival was never guaranteed.

Since White Hall, The Knife had been avoiding Pip. Still wasn't looking at him now. Instead, he glanced at Darrik. Then to Pip's dark corner.

Darrik caught the drift. "Shadow the meeting," he said. "If this turns bad, I want to know before it happens."

Pip nodded, already mapping vantage points, alley mouths, rooftops. Blacktooth's quarter was full of blind corners, tight squeezes, places to slip into shadows and stay there. He'd made a life out of it.

They moved quick, but not smooth. The Butchers that were left were either green or bought, and it showed. Weapons were checked twice, shoulders squared, glances darting — posturing to mask nerves. Nobody wanted to be the first to flinch.

The walk to the counting house was short. Neutral ground, far enough from Blacktooth's strongholds to keep things from spilling over too fast. The streets were slick with old rain, the air thick with the stink of damp wood and rusted iron. A brackish canal cut through the Slag like an open wound, black water gleaming under the weak glow of lanterns hung between leaning buildings. The Butchers moved loose, close but not huddled. Boots on uneven cobbles.

Every shadow felt like a watching eye.

The streets changed when they crossed into the Low Ward. Stone instead of wood. Sturdier buildings. But the air stayed the same — tight, waiting.

The Counting House sat at the edge of Blacktooth's turf, squat and windowless, built thick to keep out both time and thieves. Soot stains marked its facade, the heavy wooden doors strapped with iron. Above the entrance, a broken lantern swung on its last hinge, creaking in the cold breeze. The damp clung to the walls, sealing in the stink of ink, mildew, and old coin. A place meant for tallying wealth, now a battleground for something far messier.

Pip slipped away before the others entered, folding into the dark. Found a vantage point near a half-boarded window, tucked between the rotting beams of an old balcony. Good view, good cover. Eyes sharp, ears open.

Inside, The Knife took his seat at the long table. His hands twitched at his sides, too fast, too light. The kind of movement that tried too hard to look easy.

Blacktooth was already waiting, arms draped over the chair's armrests like a king at court. Behind him, his Low Dogs stood silent, their presence loud enough. Young, mean, and eager. Watching the Butchers like wolves watching a wounded pack.

Blacktooth's blackened teeth flashed as he smiled. "Knife. Good of you to come." His gaze slid to Finn, pale and silent at The Knife's side. "And I see you brought the Slag rat."

The Knife didn't answer. Just waited.

Blacktooth chuckled, leaning forward. "You know, I expected you to be stupid about this. To try and hide him, maybe. That would've made things… messier." His fingers drummed against the table. "But you came. That's good. Shows respect."

The Knife didn't blink. "I came because you called. Not because of respect."

Blacktooth's smile didn't slip. "No, I suppose not." He let that sit for a moment before exhaling slow, like this was all a game he'd already won. "Let's get to it, then. Your rat killed my kin."

His tone never changed, but the air in the room did. Heavy now. Thick.

Finn made a sound, small and broken, but didn't dare speak.

The Knife nodded his head. "And if I let him go, the debt is settled."

Blacktooth sighed, long and theatrical. "Don't play the fool, Knife." His fingers kept their slow rhythm on the table, patient. "You know a rat is not equal to kin."

He leaned back, casual, like a man with all the time in the world. "But what's fair? Maybe we talk blood for blood. Or maybe you start paying for the Slag like you want to keep it. Maybe we talk adjustments. Something between the Slag and the Low Ward. Unless you've got ideas for something better."

The words slithered between them. Not a demand, not yet. Just enough ambiguity to keep The Knife thinking, to make him wonder if maybe—just maybe—a deal could be struck. A heavy purse. A sliver of territory. A trade made from desperation.

Blacktooth let the silence stretch. Just long enough.

His smile barely there.

"Tell me, Knife. What are you offering? What do you have to offer?"

Finn blurted, "I didn't know —" but was silenced by a sharp look from The Knife.

Above, Pip shifted slightly, adjusting his position on the crumbling wooden supports. That was when he saw it — a flicker of movement in the rafters. Hidden in the deep shadows, a figure lay on the beams, crossbow braced, the bolt already drawn. The angle was clear — straight to the back of The Knife's head. A single shot, clean, silent.

Blacktooth wasn't here to bargain. He was playing with his food.

Pip moved carefully along the rafters, each step deliberate, his breath shallow. The beams creaked underfoot, but the conversation below masked any sound. The Knife leaned in slightly, his voice steady but measured. "A purse. A heavy one. Call it an understanding — one that keeps your streets from looking like the Hollow."

Blacktooth exhaled, shaking his head as if amused. "You always did think silver solved more than it does." His words were deliberate, unhurried.

The Knife's eyes flashed, but he knew he wasn't in a strong bargaining position. "We could discuss land, then. A slice of territory on the edge of the Low Ward. A shift in boundaries that favours you. More room for your crews to move."

Blacktooth smirked, his fingers still tapping against the table in that slow, lazy rhythm. "Generous. But is that all, Knife? Surely you know you've more to lose than a few streets."

The Knife paused, clearly getting frustrated. "So, tell me what you are thinking, already."

Pip had almost reached the assassin now, his form pressed low against the beams. The figure hadn't moved, his focus pinned on the men below, crossbow steady. Pip could see it clearly now — the drawn bolt, the slight tension in the assassin's stance, waiting for the moment, likely a pre-planned signal.

The Knife had no idea he was already dead.

From below, he heard oily pleasure flood through Blacktooth's voice. As the words broke the air, Pip realized what was coming, and started moving against time.

Blacktooth's voice was a blade wrapped in velvet. "What I'm thinking is that... *you'll* pay the debt."

Above, everything slowed. The assassin's fingers twitched, slowly squeezing the trigger. But Pip was already moving, and he was faster. His dagger flashed in the dim light, slicing through the air and piercing through the assassin's neck where he lay. With a solid thud, the blade stuck in the beam.

The figure barely had time to gasp. His fingers spasmed, but Pip was already on top of him, grabbing the crossbow. The bolt loosed, wild and erratic, splintering into the stone wall.

Below, Blacktooth's eyes flickered in confusion, his smirk faltering. Instinctively, his gaze jerked upward—and saw Pip, perched in the rafters, stared down at him.

For a moment, silence. The Low Dogs and Butcher stirred, hands twitching toward blades.

Pip tossed the crossbow down. Then, ripping out his knife, he kicked the body off the beam. The corpse tumbled, limbs slack, crashing down onto the table between them with a sickening thud. Blood spread across the wood, thick and dark.

The room exploded into motion.

The Knife moved first.

Fists curling, knuckles white. Shoulders back like a man readying for a blow. Then—sudden—he was on his feet, chair scraping hard against stone, fury cutting through the thick, stunned silence.

"You snake. You planned this! You think we're broken enough to bleed on command?"

Blacktooth didn't flinch. Didn't move, save for the slow curl of his fingers against the table. His face stayed unreadable, but Pip saw it—calculation, wheels turning. The plan had failed, but war wasn't the next move. Not yet.

The Knife's voice was a growl. "An assassination? That was your play?"

Blacktooth sighed, slow, measured. His smirk lingered, then faded. A flick of his eyes to the corpse sprawled across the table, then back to The Knife. Recalculating. "Come now, Knife. Be reasonable. If I wanted a war, we wouldn't be talking."

The Low Dogs bristled. The Butchers mirrored them. Hands near hilts. Shoulders tensed. One wrong move, one breath too sharp, and the counting house would run red.

The Knife saw it. Blacktooth had overreached. He hadn't planned for this. If they fought now, neither side would leave whole. And that wasn't smart business.

Blacktooth dragged his tongue slowly across his teeth, then lifted his hands, slow, palms empty. "You're angry. I understand. But you know there's nothing to gain from making this worse."

The Knife's fingers twitched. He didn't draw. Not yet. "I should gut you right here."

Blacktooth's smirk returned, just a sliver. "And you'd never leave this room. But if you walk away now, well… you live to sharpen that knife of yours another day."

A heavy silence.

Then The Knife inhaled deep. Exhaled slow. He turned, snapped his fingers once.

The Butchers hesitated—but when The Knife strode for the door, they followed.

Blacktooth didn't stop them. Didn't look at The Knife. His eyes stayed on Finn, neck red with anger. But he said nothing.

Pip didn't linger. He was already moving before the others hit the street.

---

Back in the Slag, the tension still clung to the air, thick as the stink of old blood. The Butchers filed into the Guildhouse, shaking off the weight of the meet. The Knife stood at the long table, rubbing at his jaw, lost in thought. He hesitated. Jaw tight, words caught somewhere behind his teeth.

Then, without looking at Pip, he spoke. "Good work."

Pip barely had time to register it before The Knife's gaze flicked to Darrik instead.

"For keeping eyes where they needed to be."

He didn't ask for more. And Pip didn't offer it.

# Chapter 14.    The Magistrate

Aieria had chosen Oren Fael carefully, not just for what he was, but for what he could become.

She knew his father had once been Chief Judiciar, a man steeped in the quiet, pragmatic corruption that kept Gatos running. She knew that Oren, despite being raised in that world, had rejected it. He despised the Thieves' Guild's hold on the city, had no love for the merchant lords who thought themselves kings, and had spent his career attempting to dispense real justice in a system that had no room for it. And she knew that, for all his convictions, he was still bound to the hierarchy of the courts. Grand Magistrate Beryn Tavros was his superior, and when Beryn hosted an event, Oren's attendance was not optional.

The evening was a quiet affair by Gatos' standards — too refined for the raucous gatherings of the merchant lords, too low for the grand balls of the High Ward. A space where officials, traders, and those with influence but not nobility could mingle over wine and quiet negotiations. Aieria had studied every detail of the guest list, every habit of the magistrates who would attend. She had studied Oren most of all.

Solivar was the distraction, the spectacle the room would turn to. How easily the powerful and self-important let themselves be enthralled by his charm and wit. Solivar enjoyed it, reveled in it. He would provide the opportunity to slip past unnoticed, to move where no one was looking.

The doors burst open. The bard strode in with his emerald finery and effortless charm, the room leaned toward him, as she had known it would. The magistrates and merchants, even those who sneered at his theatrics, could not resist.

While others craned their necks to see the bard, she slid in, past the nobles who would not think to look twice at a woman dressed modestly. Dark fabric, simple cut, the kind of attire that could belong to the wife of a trader or the daughter of a minor official.

Oren Fael stood near the hall's outer edges, uncomfortable among the revelry, observing the room with the trained eye of a man searching for a crime in progress. His lean frame, wrapped in the dark, practical garb of a man who valued function over finery, made him easy to overlook—a shadow against the gilded excess of the chamber. His face was angular, sharp-boned, with lines of wear etched around his eyes and mouth, the marks of years spent unraveling lies and half-truths. A streak of silver cut through his dark hair at the temples, a premature sign of the burdens he carried. He sipped from his goblet only to avoid conversation, his jaw tight, his mind elsewhere.

She approached Oren without ceremony, stepping

into the space beside him as if she had always belonged there. The warmth of the crowded room pressed against her back, the mingling scents of wine and perfumed oil thick in the air. The candlelight flickered in the polished surfaces around them, casting shifting shadows over his face, emphasizing the sharp lines of his jaw, the slight furrow of his brow. He had not yet turned to look at her, but she felt the moment he became aware of her presence — a subtle tightening of his fingers around the goblet, a shift in his breathing. He was already bracing for something unpleasant.

"Magistrate Fael," she greeted, her voice smooth, deliberate.

He turned, frowning slightly. "You have me at a disadvantage, my lady."

"Good men often are."

She had chosen her words deliberately, just as she had chosen this moment, this approach. She knew Oren Fael did not entertain empty pleasantries, that he had no tolerance for the fawning courtesies of the merchant wives or the self-indulgent musings of noblewomen who treated men like him as a curiosity. That was why she had let her voice carry weight—measured, steady, without artifice. She needed him to listen, to see her as someone worth speaking to, not another face blending into the city's endless noise. And, for the first time that night, she had his attention.

She did not meet his gaze directly, instead letting her eyes skim past him, toward the terrace doors. "Might we speak somewhere with fewer ears?"

Aieria watched him hesitate. Oren Fael was not the sort of man to step into shadows with strangers. But she also knew his instincts, his unwavering sense of caution. He would follow, not because he trusted easily, but because he understood when something was too important to ignore.

She led the way through the open doors, feeling the cool night air rush against her skin, a relief from the thick warmth of the gathering behind them. The muffled hum of conversation faded as they stepped outside, replaced by the distant lap of waves against the docks, the occasional creak of shifting wood. Here, the air was crisp, untainted by the heavy perfumes and wine-soaked breath of the event. The hush of the terrace felt vast, open—a stark contrast to the charged, suffocating atmosphere within. The lanterns lining the terrace flickered, casting long, wavering shadows against the stone. She did not turn back to see if he followed—she already knew that he would.

Once alone, she turned to face him fully, allowing the silence to stretch between them. She did not rush, did not force the moment. Instead, she let him see her— truly see her. The careful way she held herself, the weight in her gaze, the knowing patience of someone who had long since learned that recognition was inevitable. She watched as his breath stilled, his fingers tightening slightly around the goblet, the flicker of realization blooming across his face.

Aieria had not given him her name. She had not needed to. She had let him reach the conclusion himself, let the stories whispered in taverns and guarded conversations catch up to the moment standing before him. The Queen in Exile. The Fallen Daughter. A tale spoken with equal parts longing and skepticism, a myth to some, a warning to others.

And now, for Oren Fael, a reality.

His voice was quiet, but edged with something weightier than mere curiosity. "It's you."

Aieria inclined her head slightly, neither confirming nor denying, but letting him settle into the truth he had just uncovered.

"You know who I am."

Aieria saw the struggle in his eyes—the way instinct fought against reason, the way disbelief warred with the certainty settling into his bones. He wanted to reject it, to call it impossible, but she had given him no space for doubt. The pieces had already arranged themselves in his mind, the stories threading together with the weight of reality.

She held his gaze, unflinching, watching as he forced himself to breathe, to steady the shift beneath his feet. Finally, his voice came, quiet but edged with the weight of reluctant acceptance. "I know the stories."

"Stories matter, Magistrate." She stepped closer, her voice quiet but steady. "As does the truth. I have been watching you, Fael. You are one of the few who has not succumbed to the weight of this city's corruption. You fight for justice, real justice, in a place where the word itself is hollow."

His jaw tightened. "And what would you know of justice?"

Aieria did not bristle. Instead, she let a measured pause stretch between them, studying him as much as he studied her. "More than most, I think," she said at last, her voice quiet but firm. "I know what it is to have everything taken. To stand before those who believe themselves untouchable, powerless to stop them. And I know what it means to refuse to stay powerless—to fight, not for vengeance, but for something greater than oneself."

Every word was chosen carefully—not to flatter, but to align. She saw clearly the balance he maintained between his principles and survival, and she intended to tip that balance subtly in her favour.

Oren exhaled slowly, his fingers drumming once against the wooden railing. "And what do you want from me?"

"To help you."

He let out a humourless laugh. "Help me? And what could a woman in exile possibly offer that would tip the scales?"

"Knowledge. Influence. Opportunity." Her voice was steady, measured. "You want to break the Guild's hold on the courts? You need allies. You need leverage. I can give you both."

His eyes narrowed. "And why would you?"

Aieria allowed the faintest curve of her lips, not in amusement, but in understanding. "Because our goals align, Magistrate. You fight for justice in a city that has forgotten what the word means. I want to remind it. You despise Bolter because he twists the law to serve his own ends. I do not wish to see men like him hold the gavel any longer."

Aieria watched him search her face, looking for deception, for an angle she had not yet revealed. She let him. She had spoken plainly, given him no embellishments, no unnecessary persuasion—only the truth as it stood. And as she held his gaze, steady and unwavering, she saw the moment he realized there was nothing to unearth. There was no hidden play beneath her words. Only certainty.

"You are playing a dangerous game, my lady."

She met his gaze, unflinching. "No more dangerous than yours."

A long silence stretched between them.

Then, finally, "Tell me what you have in mind."

# Chapter 15.    The Guildmaster

Duke Sargo's mansion was a monument to excess, its obsidian walls glinting under the pale moon, sprawling across the cliffs of High Ward with the arrogance of old money and the smug certainty of ill-gotten wealth. It did not whisper power; it flaunted it, a fortress masquerading as civility, where influence and poison were poured into goblets with the same easy grace. The estate gleamed beneath candlelight, its polished obsidian walls and gilded reliefs glistening like a merchant's ledgers—overflowing, exaggerated, and only half-truths. Vaulted ceilings bore grand depictions of Gatos' glorious past—history so thoroughly revised it was practically a work of fiction, a tapestry of lies no less impressive for the lie.

The grand dining hall stretched long enough to host a war council, yet intimate enough to stage a betrayal over wine and venison. The air was thick with the rich aroma of roasted pheasant, the cloying sweetness of honeyed dates, and the slow, deliberate melt of wax from chandeliers so grand they could bankrupt lesser lords. Attendants moved in careful silence, refilling goblets with vintages older than some of the guests.

Solivar had tasted better from the chipped rim of a tavern flask and hadn't needed to feign gratitude for the privilege.

He swirled his goblet lazily — not in appreciation, but in boredom.

The guests — exalted in title, but hardly in worth — dripped in silks and satins dyed in the richest hues of Aierian imports, their fingers gleaming with rings stamped with seals of houses built on merchant gold, criminal enterprise, or both. Nobility in name, thieves in practice, their finery a gilded mask over refuse. The finest cutthroats in Gatos did not skulk in alleyways; they dined here, sheathed in brocade and self-importance, their daggers hidden beneath velvet smiles.

To Sargo's right sat Lord Edran Bolter, High Exalted Judiciar of the Grand Tribunal — a title so bloated with self-importance it practically required a sedan chair to carry it. He was a monument to quiet menace, his black robes so immaculately pressed they might as well have been stitched from the crushed hopes of petitioners who had once believed the Tribunal an institution of fairness. The most powerful judge in all of Durn, Lord Bolter bore the weight of his station as easily as his jeweled signet ring, his heavy-lidded stare betraying nothing. But Solivar knew the man saw everything.

To Sargo's left lounged Lady Ormella Vaedin, self-styled Keeper of the Civic Trust — an absurdity, given that trust in Gatos had long been squandered and spent. Draped in crimson and indigo, she resembled a funeral bird masquerading as a peacock, her fingers so heavy with rings it was a wonder she could lift her goblet. She was a woman who had never known hunger and had ensured that others did.

Beside her sat Lord Castian Relmar, the quiet sovereign of Gatos' ports, his control so complete that even the seagulls likely had to bribe him for a place to land. Half the city's illicit goods passed through his ledgers with the grace of a blessing, the other half with the full knowledge that displeasing him meant an unplanned, permanent swim. He wore his station well, his doublet stitched with thread-of-gold in the shape of curling waves. Solivar had yet to decide whether the man was more shark or barnacle. Likely the latter — though even barnacles had a way of clinging to power long past their welcome.

A servant bent to refill Relmar's goblet, and the Lord of the Ports waved him off with the absent flick of a man who had long ceased to acknowledge the existence of those who served him. A moment later, he was leaning toward Vaedin, murmuring something low and conspiratorial. She laughed — high and brittle, a glass too thin to withstand the weight of its own indulgence.

Sargo himself sat like a lion draped in gold, a predator at rest but never at ease. His brocade coat gleamed beneath the chandelier's glow, the filigree a needless vanity for a man who had no need to *prove* his power. He was Duke by title, Guildmaster in truth, the hand that tightened the noose around Gatos' throat with practiced ease. The Red Knives moved at his command, the streets bled for his favour, and the coin flowed only because he willed it. Around him, the city's elite feigned camaraderie, trading empty pleasantries like merchants haggling over counterfeit relics. They all knew better. Beneath their velvet and jewels, their survival was measured in Sargo's whims.

Solivar, however, was neither merchant nor viper. He was an artist. He had been invited, he had sung, and for the length of a song, that made him important.

The evening had settled into its usual, dull rhythm — meaningless courtesies exchanged over too-rich wine, the occasional chime of a knife against porcelain — when the doors opened.

Viktor Durnvale — *Blacktooth*, gods help us, that was the name he chose — strode in with the confidence of a man who had not yet learned that confidence could get you killed. His coat was damp from the night air, his heavy boots leaving small, defiant imprints upon the polished marble floor. He did not bow, nor did he offer the usual simpering flatteries.

Oh, but grief made men reckless.

"Duke," Blacktooth said, inclining his head just enough to be polite without debasing himself. "A moment."

Sargo lifted a hand, lazily swirling his wine, the movement unhurried, indulgent. "For what, Viktor?

You interrupt my dinner. This must be terribly important."

"In private."

Sargo sighed; the sound languid, almost bored — though Solivar knew better. There was curiosity beneath the act, sharp as a dagger beneath silk. But power was never shown in haste. So, Sargo took his time, let the silence stretch just long enough for the weight of his indulgence to press upon Blacktooth's shoulders. Then, with the easy grace of a man who had never known the taste of fear, he rose from his seat, setting his goblet down without a sound.

"You do know how I hate interruptions," he murmured, adjusting the cuffs of his coat with idle precision. He cast a knowing glance at Bolter, the silent assurance that the dinner would continue in his absence.

They moved toward the hall as Solivar took his place upon the small stage. His fingers danced over the strings of his lute, plucking a few idle notes, feigning distraction while his ears remained sharp. The advantage of being overlooked was that no one ever thought to lower their voices around a bard. He had built his career upon words not meant for him, and tonight would be no different.

The great dining chamber still hummed with conversation, but a subtle, delicious tension coiled at the far end where Duke Sargo now stood with

Blacktooth. Solivar shifted slightly, just enough to appear immersed in his own world, while the Duke's low voice carried through the vaulted space.

"Say what you came to say, Viktor." Sargo's voice was casual, rich with indulgent boredom, as though humouring a petitioner rather than addressing a man with murder in his eyes.

Blacktooth's jaw tightened. "My cousin, you remember him?"

"Sure. That big one with the broken nose?" Sargo swirled his wine, watching the candlelight catch in its depths. "No, the scrawny one who always smelled like fish. Or was it the drunk? The one with the lisp?"

Blacktooth's fingers twitched. He forced them to unclench. "Goldtooth. The one you sometimes mistook for a different cousin."

"Ah. Yes." A lazy smile played at the corner of Sargo's mouth.

"He's dead. One of the Knife's new recruits—a whelp named Finn—cut his throat in the street."

Sargo took a slow sip of wine before responding. "And?"

Blacktooth inhaled sharply, steadying himself. "And The Knife refuses to hand him over."

Sargo gave a long, thoughtful hum, his expression unreadable. "Not quite the way I heard it, Viktor."

Blacktooth hesitated. A tell. There was always something satisfying about watching men like Blacktooth realize they were holding bad cards. Less satisfying when they realized it too slowly.

"I heard you figured you might deal with The Knife yourself. On a permanent basis."

Blacktooth stiffened. "That wasn't—"

"Save it," Sargo interrupted, voice deceptively mild. "I know about your botched assassination. Careless, Viktor."

"It was the kid," Blacktooth insisted, voice rising. "Not you—"

"Maybe I believe you." Sargo tilted his head, studying him. "Maybe not." He let the silence stretch just long enough for unease to creep in. "In any event, The Knife can't keep this Finn inside forever. Be patient."

"It's not just that." Blacktooth's voice dropped lower, tension creeping into his shoulders. "There's a problem."

Sargo arched a brow. "What is it?"

Blacktooth hesitated, then exhaled, as if saying it aloud might make it real. "You remember that kid the Knife found in the gutter? Pip? They say he isn't just some gutter rat no more. He's turned into something. Something unnatural. Say he moves like a ghost, that he sees things before they happen. I sent a couple in to carve Finn out of that hole, and three of them didn't come back. The one that did…" His throat bobbed as he recalled the man's wide, vacant eyes. "Wouldn't stop shaking. He talked about shadows that kill, knives they never saw coming."

Solivar's fingers slowed over the lute strings.

Sargo, however, merely scoffed. But for the briefest moment, something passed through his expression—an almost imperceptible shift, gone before it could be named. "For this? Ghost stories, and the loss of your men's nerve? For this, you interrupt my dinner?"

Blacktooth's composure frayed. His mouth opened, then closed. He shook his head, muttering something under his breath before finally forcing himself to say it.

"They say it wasn't just skill," he admitted, his voice lower now, as if speaking too loudly might summon something unseen. "It wasn't just luck. It was… wrong. *Unnatural.*"

Sargo exhaled, long-suffering. "Oh, for the love of the gods, Viktor—"

"I know how it sounds," Blacktooth snapped, his control slipping. "And I don't give a damn. Three of my men went in, and only one came out, babbling nonsense about shadows that move on their own, about seeing their own deaths before they happened." He swallowed hard. "And now, none of the boys will go into the Slag alone."

Solivar's fingers slowed over the lute strings. *Well, well.* Now *that* was interesting. A chill of recognition slithered down his spine, settling somewhere behind his ribs. Ghost stories had their place, of course—he had spun a few himself when the moment demanded—but true fear, when genuine, never needed embellishment. And Blacktooth? He wasn't telling a tale. His words carried no art, no flair for dramatics. This wasn't a man spinning fables. That, more than anything, made it worth listening to.

Sargo let the silence stretch, watching Blacktooth the way a jeweler might examine a flawed gemstone—measuring its worth, deciding whether to polish or discard it. His expression was unreadable, but Solivar had spent too many nights in rooms just like this one to mistake that stillness for disinterest.

Finally, Sargo exhaled, long and slow. "So, what do you want, Viktor?"

Blacktooth stepped forward, shoulders squaring as he steadied his voice. "I need to handle this before it festers. We can't have men refusing to walk their own streets." A pause—brief, calculated—before he softened his tone, schooling his anger into something more palatable. "I'll make it quiet. No spectacle. No loose ends."

Sargo leaned back slightly, drawing out the pause like a cat watching a trapped bird struggle. And then, with the weight of absolute certainty, he spoke.

"No."

Blacktooth bristled. "He's weak. This won't spark a war."

The Duke didn't even *look* at him. He adjusted the cuffs of his coat with deliberate care, smoothing the fine silk, his manner languid, indulgent. When he finally deigned to respond, his voice carried the same unhurried certainty.

"No."

A breath. The tension stretched thin between them. Blacktooth's jaw tightened. "No?"

Sargo did not blink. "I ordered the turf wars finished. The Guild back to business. And you assume The Knife is weak, but a cornered dog is a dangerous thing."

Blacktooth's voice frayed at the edges. "You're going to let my cousin's killer walk?"

Sargo took his time, lifting his goblet, rolling the stem between his fingers. When he smiled, it was almost *indulgent.* "Did I say that?"

The air in the room shifted, the conversation settling into something colder, sharper. Blacktooth's mouth tightened. He had been dismissed. The Duke had decided, and there would be no shifting the weight of his will.

Sargo's smile lingered. "Stay. Eat. Drink. Listen to the bard. It will cheer your spirits."

Blacktooth's fists curled at his sides. He exhaled sharply through his nose, as if biting back words best left unsaid. For a heartbeat, it looked as though he might say *something*—one final defiance, a parting shot—but he swallowed it. With effort, he forced his shoulders to ease, unclenched his jaw, and stepped back. "Duke." The word was clipped. An acknowledgment, not a submission. He turned on his heel and stalked from the hall, his boots ringing hollow against the stone.

The doors shut behind him with the finality of a book snapping closed.

Sargo exhaled softly, amused. He turned back to the table, settling into his chair beside the High Judiciar with the ease of a man who had never truly been challenged. Lifting his goblet, he took a slow, measured sip, then leaned toward Bolter. His voice dropped low—but not low enough.

"Have Malren round this Finn up."

Bolter listened, impassive, then gave a single nod.

Sargo rolled the stem of his goblet between his fingers, as though the decision meant nothing, as though he had just chosen which wine to pour. And then, turning back to the conversation, he murmured one last thing—just loud enough for Solivar to catch the whisper of it.

"Try him. Finish him."

Solivar exhaled, slow and measured, letting his gaze drift from Sargo to Bolter. He took a sip of wine, suppressing a smile.

A song was forming—one of knives in the dark, of ghosts that did not stay buried. And for the first time that evening, he was no longer bored.

# Chapter 16.    The Weight of Scales

The magistrate's chambers smelled of ink and old parchment, of dust and decisions left to yellow with time. Shelves sagged beneath the weight of tomes no one had opened in years, their laws as brittle as their bindings. The desk at the room's centre was a fortress of paper, its surface a battlefield of unfinished judgments and half-signed orders. Wax seals lay broken, their authority spent. It was the scent of power in stagnation.

Magistrate Oren Fael sat behind that desk, his shoulders hunched under the weight of his duties, his quill scratching with the meticulous strokes of a man who still believed the ink he spilled could shape the world. He was a rare thing in Port Gatos — honourable. Honourable enough to be frustrated. Honourable enough to be useful.

He didn't look up as she approached, though the tightening of his fingers around the quill told her he was acutely aware of her presence. He was measuring the moment, deciding how much power to grant her simply by meeting her gaze. Aieria knew the weight of names, knew how hers had once commanded rooms. Now, she was a relic seated before a man who still had a place in the world, and he wanted her to feel that shift. She did not let him see if it stung. Aieria knew the game. She had played it before, had let silence test her, weigh her, attempt to make her shift beneath its weight.

She did not shift.

Instead, she smiled. "If I thought you a fool, I would not be here."

That earned his attention. The quill paused. He set it down, fingers steepling as he leaned back. "Then speak."

She did not waste time, her voice steady but edged with urgency. "A man has been arrested under false charges. Extortion of a high lady, they claim."

Fael exhaled sharply, a sound that carried the weight of too many battles fought and lost, though whether in irritation or expectation, she could not tell. "And which poor soul have our esteemed courts decided to make an example of this time?"

"His name is Chally Finn. He is connected to the Butchers." She saw the flicker in his expression, the instinctual recoil at the Guild association, but she pressed on. "Yes, but not guilty of *this* crime. The charge is not about justice. It is a move against the Slag's Quartermaster, Havrin "The Knife" Moru, a performance of loyalty to the Guildmaster — by none other than your High Exalted Judiciar of the Grand Tribunal, Lord Edran Bolter."

There. That name hit its mark. Fael's jaw tightened, his hands pressing flat against the desk as if to steady himself, the weight of Bolter's reputation pressing down on him like a stone. There was no need to elaborate on Lord Bolter's reputation. It dripped from his very title, the Chief Judiciar's authority less a matter of law than of purchase. Aieria saw the way Fael swallowed, saw the quiet storm that gathered in his expression. He already knew what she was telling him. He had always known.

He shook his head. "If the case is already moving, there is little I can do. The accused will be taken before the Lower Court, and as you may know, I do not preside there."

Aieria remained unruffled. "But you have influence. And more than that, you have friends."

Fael studied her, but not as a stranger. His gaze was sharper, weighted, as if searching for the Queen she once had been, a flicker of recognition in his eyes that spoke of battles fought and lost. She stood before him, stripped of her throne, her crown, her name. His lips pressed together, and in his expression, she caught something close to sorrow—or was it disappointment?

"You shouldn't be here," he murmured. Not a warning. A truth.

She let the words settle but did not answer them.

Fael was weighing his choices, and she let him. Frustration was a dangerous thing in a man like him, a man who had once believed in something greater than himself. If tempered well, it could turn into action.

He exhaled, rubbing his chin. "Master Helbric Torven is the head of the Lower Court. We've known each other for years. If anyone might listen, it is him."

She inclined her head. "And will he?"

Fael let out a dry chuckle, but there was little humour in it. His fingers curled into a loose fist. A small, controlled gesture, but one that betrayed the irritation simmering beneath his measured exterior. He leaned back, blowing out slowly, the motion stiff—calculating. This was not just frustration; it was the weight of knowing exactly how deep the rot ran, and how little power he had to carve it out. "Oh, he'll listen. But if I bring this to him, he will want proof."

"The charges will land on his desk. Any proof of guilt will not."

Fael let out a slow breath. "Of course not." He leaned back in his chair, gaze distant as he considered. The silence stretched, heavy with possibility. Then, he tapped a finger against his desk. "There is something… a precedent, though rarely used."

Aieria arched a brow, waiting.

"In cases of great public interest, the accused can be tried in the Gallows Square," he said. "Most often, these are theatrical—trials in name only, meant to appease the crowd before the sentence is carried out. But…" He tilted his head, considering. "If Torven were to preside himself, he could ensure a real trial takes place."

She saw it then in his eyes—a flicker of something rare. A moment, however brief, where the law could do what it was meant to do.

Aieria smiled, slow and deliberate. "One small act of justice. One small defiance against the Thieves Guild's rule."

Fael's lips pressed together, his fingers drumming against the wood. He was a man who had spent too long watching the rot spread. A man who wanted— needed—to believe that something could still be salvaged.

Finally, he nodded. "I will speak with Torven."

Aieria dipped her head in thanks, careful not to let triumph show. This was not about Finn. Not really. This was about the long game. About pushing Fael forward, undermining Bolter piece by piece. One trial would not shake the city. But it was a beginning.

# Chapter 17.    A Word in the Dark

Aieria had chosen her garments with the precision of a blade being sharpened. The cloak, deep as the sky before dawn, was not merely fabric but an intention—rich enough to suggest standing, unembellished enough to avoid scrutiny. The cut was tailored but loose, a shape meant to obscure rather than define. It flowed with her movements, silent, measured, purposeful. It was thick, lined with a heavier weave beneath, suited for the chill of the night but more importantly for obscuring the shape of her frame. The hood draped forward, heavy enough to swallow the candlelight, leaving only the glint of her eyes visible in its depths. Beneath it, a veil of fine black silk lay against her skin, delicate yet impenetrable, masking her features while allowing breath and whispered words to pass unnoticed. It was not only concealment—it was control. It was a delicate balance—she needed to look important enough to command respect, but not so grand as to be remembered.

Indaros stood beside her, his dark attire unadorned, built for function rather than display. He had warned her against this meeting, his voice tight with disapproval, but she had overruled him. The game required risk, and risk was something she had always been willing to take.

The footsteps arrived before the figures did—

measured, deliberate, men who knew how to move without drawing notice. The door creaked open, and two entered.

Stone entered first. He was built like a man who had spent his life earning his reputation the hard way — stocky, powerful, a frame hardened by years of breaking bones and collecting debts. The bulk of him wasn't wasted mass; it was the kind of strength that could pin a man against a wall and make him listen. His face was square-cut, his jaw firm, shadowed by dark stubble that never fully faded. A scar cut through his left brow, another traced the line of his jaw, each a story no doubt. His dark hair was cropped short, kept practical rather than stylish. His leathers, reinforced at the shoulders and elbows, bore the wear of a man who had walked through too many fights to keep count. A single broad blade rested at his hip, a weapon that had seen just as much work as his fists. When he stepped forward, his boots pressed firm against the wood — not soundless, but deliberate, the tread of a man who didn't need silence to make people fear him.

Behind him, a shadow followed.

A ripple of discomfort prickled her skin. The young man who accompanied Stone was slight, wiry, dressed in nondescript garb chosen for practicality rather than vanity. But something was profoundly wrong about him, something that made her pulse tighten, her instincts recoil. The air around him felt stretched thin. He was small, wiry, built for slipping through spaces where men should not fit, but his presence carried a weight that had nothing to do with muscle. He did not just move—he slid, like shadow and intent made flesh, a thing poised on the edge of action, waiting for the moment to unravel. His features were sharp, almost delicate, foxlike in their quickness, but it was his eyes that rooted her to the spot—dark and empty as death. They did not just see; they consumed, peeling away layers with the slow inevitability of something ancient wearing the face of a boy. This was the thing they whispered of in the Low Ward—the shadow that even the Low Dogs feared, the presence that made hardened killers hesitate. Pip. The name felt insufficient, too small for what stood before her.

Aieria let out a breath she hadn't meant to hold. She had met dangerous men before. But this was something else.

Stone gave Indaros a slow, knowing nod.

"Thought you were dead," Stone remarked.

"You should be so lucky," Indaros shot back.

There was the faintest ghost of a smirk on Stone's face before he turned his attention back to Aieria.

"And you're the dress who thinks she can play in our streets."

Indaros stiffened beside her, his posture sharpening like a blade drawn from its sheath. His fingers twitched, weighing the worth of a response, but Aieria waved him down.

She met Stone's gaze, unflinching. "I'm the dress telling you that Chally Finn is about to be arrested and hung."

Stone exhaled, unimpressed. "And?"

She tilted her head, but the ease was forced now, something brittle at the edges. "And unless you want to see him paraded through the streets in chains, he needs to disappear." The words felt heavier in her mouth than they should have. To her, it was a life — messy, flawed, but a life. To Stone, it was an inconvenience, something to be discarded without a second thought. The casual weight of his indifference unsettled her more than she let show.

Stone folded his arms across his broad chest, shifting his weight slightly, settling. "You come down here in your pretty get-up to tell me that? If the Watch is after him, they've already decided. Doesn't much matter what we do."

"No, that's The Knife's problem. And yours, if you have any sense." Her voice was smooth, deliberate, but there was an edge beneath it, a quiet force pressing against his certainty.

Stone scoffed. "You think the Butchers start shaking just because the hounds come sniffing?"

She stepped forward, the movement sharp, precise —

a shift from careful persuasion to controlled force. She could feel herself slipping, losing ground, losing control. The weight of his indifference, the sheer immovability of his stance, pressed against her like a closing door. She had one move left. If he wouldn't listen to words, she would make him listen to truth.

Her voice dropped, not soft, but heavy with certainty. "Finn killed Goldtooth. Accident or not, that left a debt. Maybe The Knife would've paid, maybe not — but Blacktooth made his choice when he tried to have The Knife killed. After that, the debt didn't matter. But now Sargo's stepping in, and he isn't interested in who was right. He just wants the blood settled and the streets quiet."

She let that sink in, then continued.

"Bolter's orders are clear. The Watch will take Finn. If The Knife fights them, they'll take him, too. That's not a warning, it's a certainty."

Stone didn't shift, but she saw the flicker of thought behind his eyes. He was weighing her, measuring not just the truth in her words, but the fact that she had them at all. Some of this he knew, but now she was proving she wasn't just another outsider playing at understanding their world — she had stepped inside it, walked through its shadows, and returned with knowledge she was not supposed to have. And that, more than anything, was what made him listen.

"But if Finn vanishes? If the Watch show up and he's

nowhere to be found? Then they lean on The Knife, but they don't get their fight. They don't get to drag him through the streets. And your boss still gets to spit in Blacktooth's eye."

Stone's eyes narrowed, measuring her differently now. Not just some noblewoman playing at knowing the streets.

Aieria pressed. "You tell me which of those sounds like the better outcome."

Finally, he asked what she had been waiting for. "Why do you care?"

Aieria met his gaze without hesitation. "I don't care about Finn. But there are men who will be embarrassed if he slips through their fingers. And embarrassed men make bad decisions. That's useful to me."

Stone's brow furrowed, suspicion still lacing his features. "And why should I believe you?"

She smiled, cool and composed. "Because it costs me nothing to warn you. But it'll cost you a hell of a lot more if you ignore me."

Stone studied her a moment longer, then nodded. "I'll see that he hears it."

Aieria inclined her head. "Make sure he does."

# Chapter 18.   Marshal Jon Malren

The note had been too clean.

*The Duke suspects.*

*Your daughter is not safe.*

*We should talk.*

Unsigned. Simple. Elegant. No unnecessary words. Just enough to shake Malren's well-ordered world, to crack the foundation he had stood upon for a decade.

The note had been delivered to Jon Malren, Marshal of the City Watch—the highest-ranking officer in Gatos' law enforcement. He had spent days chasing the whisper to its source, calling in favours, pressing informants, even attempting to track the note's origin through the Watch's own channels. But every path led nowhere. Every question was met with silence that only grew heavier. He dared not go near the Red Knives—Sargo's patience was not something to test, not when the subject was his daughter. Malren knew better than to invite suspicion; the wrong question in the wrong ear could mark the beginning of his ruin.

As he worked, she watched.

Aieria had followed his movements without ever stepping into his sight. She had seen him lean too close to an informant in a candlelit tavern, his voice calm, but his fingers restless. She had noted the way he moved through the halls of the City Watch, careful, methodical—hiding his concern behind the mask of a man merely ensuring order. Even the way he returned home, later than usual, wary of his own footsteps, did not escape her.

She let him breathe. She waited until the time was right, when his panic had started to fade, when he had almost convinced himself that he was imagining things. Let him settle back into routine, let him believe—for just long enough—that his fears had been baseless. That he had overestimated the danger. That the world had not, in fact, shifted beneath him.

Only then was it time.

Aieria placed the second message where it could not be ignored—a single folded scrap, slipped beneath the silver tray at his favourite dining house, waiting for him like an old friend. She did not watch him retrieve it, nor did she need to. Indaros, stationed in the shadows near the door, gave the barest tilt of his head when it was done—confirmation enough.

She had chosen the moment with care, ensuring he was relaxed, his mind momentarily freed from the gnawing weight of suspicion. The handwriting was unmistakable—elegant, deliberate, with a precision that mirrored the careful control she wielded. Three lines again, written in dark ink, pressed into fine parchment:

———

*Tonight.*

*The Ember Vault.*

*Midnight.*

———

The Vault had once been a place of function, its walls lined with racks of weapons, shelves stacked with ledgers and records no one outside the City Watch was ever meant to see. But time had swallowed its purpose, leaving only dust and forgotten crates, their edges softened by years of neglect. The floor was uneven, worn smooth in some places by the boots of long-departed watchmen, while in others, dampness crept through the cracks. The air was thick with the scent of oil from the lanterns that barely pushed back the darkness, mingling with the stale musk of aged parchment and rot.

The Ember Vault did not exist on any official ledger. It was a place swallowed by time and left to be forgotten—the perfect setting for a conversation no one could afford be overheard.

Her garments were finely tailored but muted, a dark

blue cloak fastened with a simple silver clasp, the hood drawn up to hide her face. Beneath, a fitted tunic of deep charcoal cinched at the waist, the cut deliberate — neither ostentatious nor forgettable. Her gloves were supple black leather, her boots silent against the stone. Nothing about her was excessive, nothing a distraction. The power in this encounter would not come from how she looked, but from how she carried herself. Measured, composed, untouchable.

When he arrived, Aieria sat at the far end of the empty chamber, framed by the amber glow of a lantern swaying gently from a rusted chain.

She did not look at him as he entered, nor did she move. She simply waited.

She heard him hesitate. He had spent his life navigating power, knowing when to bow and when to press. But here, in this moment, he was stripped of control before he had spoken a word.

After moment she heard his steps approaching with resolve. She remained still.

"You went to a great deal of trouble to arrange this meeting." His voice was measured, careful, but she could hear what lay beneath — the anger that masked fear, the way his body braced against the vulnerability he refused to acknowledge. "I suppose I should be impressed."

She let the silence press in, allowed him to fill it first.

He exhaled, stepping forward. "What do you know?"

Aieria turned her head then, shifting just enough for the lantern's glow to catch the edge of her features, her eyes meeting his from within the hood's shadow. She did not let satisfaction touch her expression, nor amusement. She wanted him to see nothing he could fight against — only the weight of certainty.

"Your daughter should not suffer for your mistakes."

It was not a threat. Not an accusation. Just a fact.

She could see his mind racing, the frantic calculations behind his eyes. He was sifting through his options, testing the weight of each before discarding them — denial, too thin; deflection, too transparent; control, already lost. She watched the moment he realized that every plan he had prepared, every maneuver he might have used, was useless here. The panic tightened in his throat, but his pride forced it down, smoothing his face, steadying his breath. Yet she had already seen it — the fracture beneath the surface, the knowledge that he was caught, and there was no path forward that did not lead to ruin.

She let the weight of her knowledge settle over him, closing off his options before he could even see them. Every instinct told him to push back, to bargain — but she had already sealed every exit. There was nowhere left to go.

"The Duke is searching for answers. He won't stop. And if he finds the truth," she asked, tilting her head, "what happens next?"

"He won't find anything."

The words were too quick, too forceful. Aieria caught the flicker of panic behind them. He hadn't denied the affair — he hadn't even tried. Instead, his instinct had been to control the damage, to shut the door before it could be forced open. But by doing so, he had already proven that the truth was inside.

"Because you'll stop him?" Her voice didn't change, but she saw the way the question landed — heavy, final, a door slamming shut. She had given him no room to pretend, no path to sidestep the truth. Killing the Guildmaster was impossible. Malren knew it. She knew it. And by putting the thought in his head, by forcing him to face its absurdity, she sealed him inside the only option left to him. He was caught, and they both knew it.

It wasn't a question. It was inevitability, spoken aloud.

His breath sharpened, his fingers curling into a fist. For a moment, he stood frozen in the tightening snare of her words, the full weight of his entrapment settling into his ribs. Then instinct overrode reason. A last, desperate move. His hand shot for the sword at his hip. A breath. A blur.

Indaros moved faster.

The blade barely made it past its sheath. A sharp sound—metal against stone—as it was wrenched from Malren's grip and sent clattering across the floor. Then impact. A forceful, bone-jarring thud as Indaros drove the big man back against the stone wall. The air left Malren's lungs in a choked gasp, his body folding under the sudden, inescapable weight of Indaros' grip.

Aieria did not move. She only watched.

Malren twitched, his limbs struggling for control, his breath coming in short, pained bursts as his ribs buckled under the force of the blow. But there had been no real fight. No struggle. Just inevitability.

She waited. Waited for the anger to drain from his limbs, for the moment his body sagged in Indaros' grip, the weight of his own failure pressing down on him. When it came—when she saw the flicker of recognition in his eyes, the moment he truly understood just how trapped he was—she stepped forward, her footsteps quiet against the stone.

She lowered her voice, let the words settle into him like iron. "What do you think happens to your perfect life," she asked, "when Gatos learns that your success was built on a lie? That your greatest ally was a woman who never loved her husband, but you?"

The words hollowed him. It was not just about the affair. If the truth spread, the Duke would demand his head. The Duchess—his Duchess—would be ruined, her influence shattered, all because of a mistake they made a decade ago. And worst of all—his daughter. She would be cast out, disowned, discarded as a stain upon noble blood. Sargo did not forgive betrayal, and he certainly did not tolerate the illusion of weakness.

Aieria studied him for a moment and then nodded. He knew she had won. She did not gloat, did not press him further. She merely offered him a way out.

"Collapse is a choice, Malren. Stability, however, can be arranged." She let the words settle, offering him not a threat, but a truth he could not afford to ignore.

She turned then, moving past him. She could have left him there, but instead, she paused just long enough to deliver the final blow.

"If a warrant is issued for Lord Edran Bolter, Malren, just do your duty. No escape."

And with that, she was gone.

# Chapter 19.    The Price of Loyalty

The private chamber in the guildhall was dimly lit, the heavy scent of pipe smoke curling through the stagnant air. A single candle flickered on the battered table where The Knife sat, legs sprawled, fingers drumming idly against the wood. The room was close, thick with heat, and silence reigned but for the occasional creak of a chair or the shuffle of a restless foot. Shadows stretched long against the stone walls, cast by the shifting glow of the flame, making the place feel smaller than it was.

Pip kept to the shadows, as he always did, watching, listening. Darrik stood before The Knife, hands loose at his sides, stance easy—but Pip caught the way his fingers twitched now and then. Darrik had news, and the kind of news that made a man cautious about how he delivered it.

"Indaros set it up," Darrik said, his voice casual, but with the measured weight of a man reporting something that mattered. "Met with some lady out of the High Ward."

The Knife raised a brow, tilting his head back slightly. "Indaros? The same Indaros who fell face-first into a bed with that pirate woman? Gods, she was something, wasn't she? All curves and sharp teeth. What was her name?" He waved a lazy hand, pretending to search his memory. "Ah, never mind.

Doesn't matter. Indaros was a fool for her. He's always had a weakness for women."

"Still does," Darrik muttered. "Looks like he's moved up in the world, though. Seems he's playing at being a bodyguard now."

The Knife snorted. "And who is he protecting?"

"Name she gave was Lady Elsera Valtren," Darrik said. "Made-up, of course. But she's got the airs for it. Dresses like a noble. Talks like one. Full of herself, if you ask me. Real piece of work. Fancy. Arrogant. Beautiful. The kind of woman who'd make a man forget his good sense. And Indaros? Poor bastard's already trailing after her like a dog on a leash."

The Knife's smirk faded slightly, his fingers stilling against the wood. "What did she want?"

Darrik's grin thinned. "Sent a message. Said there's a warrant out for Finn. Came straight from Sargo, she says. Wanted you to know."

Silence stretched, thick as tar. Pip watched The Knife's expression shift, the easy smirk fading as something heavier settled behind his eyes. Sargo wanted Finn dead. Not roughed up. Not exiled. Dead. That meant something. It wasn't just a grudge, wasn't just politics—it was a line drawn, a name crossed out before the ink had dried.

Darrik was still several steps behind. "What do you want us to do? Hide Finn? Get him out of the city?

Maybe he could make a go of it with the Black Bough in the Mirewood."

The Knife considered that, gaze flicking between Darrik and Pip. Pip held still. He knew where this was going before The Knife even spoke.

"No."

Surprise flickered in Darrik's eyes. "No?"

The Knife showed teeth, shaking his head. "Finn gets handed over. It's a blood debt. It should be paid, and it would have been paid if Blacktooth hadn't tried to shoot me in the back. If Sargo wants him dead, he dies. Saves me the trouble of doing it myself. Avoids a war. Keeps the peace. And, frankly, Finn deserves what's coming to him."

He leaned back in his chair, stretching out as if the matter was already settled. "Let Malren know it's safe to come get Finn."

Darrik hesitated, as if he wanted to argue but thought better of it. Pip watched him from the corner of his eye. The tension in the room had changed — not loud, not obvious, but it was there, a shift in the air, a hesitation that hadn't been present before.

The Knife tapped his fingers against the table in thought, then looked back to Pip, eyes dark with meaning. "Make sure Finn doesn't run."

Pip gave the slightest nod, understanding the weight

behind the words.

The Knife sighed, stretching his fingers. "And one more thing—this Lady Valtren." He said the name with disdain, like something bitter on his tongue. "I don't like people knowing our business. Find out who she really is, where she comes from, what she wants, and why she's sticking her nose where it don't belong. Get it from Indaros if you can—nicely." He cast a glance at Pip, a flicker of something darker in his smirk. "Or the other way. I don't care. Just get me the information."

Darrik shifted again. "You think she's trouble?"

The Knife leaned forward slightly, his grin widening in a way that wasn't quite friendly. "She's either trouble or she's useful. And if she's neither, she's a corpse waiting to happen."

Pip didn't need to be told twice. If this Lady Valtren knew too much, she wouldn't be a problem for long.

The Knife stood then, stretching as if the conversation had bored him. He stepped past Pip and Darrik toward a small cabinet against the far wall, pulling out a bottle and three cups. "Drink?" he asked, voice light, conversational, as if he hadn't just sentenced a man to die.

Darrik took a cup without a word. Pip hesitated for half a second before accepting. The Knife poured, the liquid sloshing into each glass, rich and dark. He lifted his own in a lazy salute. "To orders followed.

To debts paid."

Darrik drank first. Pip followed. The Knife knocked his back in one gulp, setting the cup down with a sharp *clack* against the wood.

Then he smirked, turning back toward the room beyond, where his Butchers waited, unaware their comrade's fate had just been sealed. "Now," he murmured, "let's get Finn ready for his farewell."

# Chapter 20.    The Cut of the Knife

The Butchers' Guildhouse smelled of blood and wet wood, the scent of old violence sunk deep into the beams. The front room was wide and open, the kind of space meant for work that left stains.

Pip stood behind Finn, arms loose at his sides, gaze steady. The weight of the moment pressed against his ribs; the kind of tension that made a man check his exits without moving his head. This wasn't a fight yet, but it was close enough to taste. Finn wasn't moving. Hadn't twitched since the Watch stepped in, their numbers filling the room like an overstuffed corpse.

The Butchers stood in loose formation, the stink of sweat and steel thick in the air. Some leaned against the wooden posts, arms folded, fingers tapping idly against knife handles, while others stood ready, weight balanced, their eyes flicking between The Knife and the Watch like dogs waiting for the command to tear into a meal. The tension hummed just beneath the surface, the kind that could turn sharp with a single word.

The Watch held their ground. Their uniforms were clean but worn, the sheen of oil and damp clinging to their boots. They didn't fidget, didn't shift like the Butchers did. They stood as if the law still meant something in this place, even if everyone knew better.

At their head stood the Marshal, a man as weathered and unyielding as the city's oldest stone. His face betrayed nothing—no disgust, no nerves, no patience for the spectacle playing out before him. A Watchman stepped forward, parchment in hand, clearing his throat to read the charges. Marlen reached out a large hand and firmly pushed the scroll down with finality. "You needn't bother with that," Marlen said flatly.

The Knife straightened his shoulders, tilting his head just enough to cast his smirk over the gathered Butchers, letting them see the ease in his stance, the confidence in his grin. He was the biggest man in the room, and he wanted them all to know it. He gave the Marshal a slow once-over, eyes dragging down and back up, as if weighing the man and finding him lacking. "Must be nice," he mused, "walking in here with the whole City Watch at your back. Not much of a spine left under that uniform, is there, Malren?"

Pip didn't move. He watched. He waited. That was his job.

Finn trembled, breath coming too fast, too shallow. His shoulders tensed like a man trying to shrink into himself, to disappear before the noose could find his neck. Pip remained a shadow at his back, silent, watchful. Finn wouldn't run. He didn't dare.

The Marshal spoke with patience. Just a man doing

his job. "Knife, you know Finn's coming with us. Let's end this now before your posturing wastes any more of our evening."

The Knife strolled forward, easy as anything, spreading his arms as if welcoming old friends. "Oh, I would, if you didn't make it impossible to say nothing. But these charges, though! Extortion of a high lady?" He barked a laugh, shaking his head, his grin widening as he turned back to his men, playing to the room. "Tell me, Malren, do you say it with a straight face? Or does it take everything in you not to choke on the words?" He let the moment linger before looking back at the Marshal, eyes sharp with amusement. "Finn wouldn't be that stupid. And you aren't that stupid either, are you? Coming in here, parading your authority, when everyone in this room knows exactly what this is." His voice dropped slightly, the sneer deepening. "We know these charges are a farce."

The Marshal's expression didn't flicker. "We do," he said. "And yet here I am."

The Knife sneered, rolling his shoulders with slow, deliberate ease, as if shaking off an irritating thought. His smirk lingered a beat too long, a lazy thing that curled at the edges, like a man savouring a private joke no one else was in on. "Bootlickers, the lot of you. Bowing and scraping for scraps like whipped dogs. Tell me, Malren, does it ever get tiring? Having your leash yanked whenever Bolter so much as twitches? Does he let you off long enough to piss, or does he make you ask permission first?"

A few of the gathered Watch looked away, jaws tightening. No one spoke.

Malren remained impassive. He didn't need to argue. He had the numbers, the city, the law — bought and twisted as it was.

"And yet, here you stand, Marshal. Dragging your boots through my hall, barking orders." The Knife took a casual step forward, closing the space between them. The Watch didn't move at first, but as he neared, a few hands twitched toward hilts, shoulders tensing.

The Knife rolled his shoulders, still smiling, letting the silence stretch, savoring the weight of the moment. He glanced at his men, making sure they saw it — the easy confidence, the unshaken amusement, the sense that he owned the space they all stood in. He ran a hand over his jaw as if considering something, then exhaled slow, shaking his head like a man burdened by fools. The smirk deepened, a lazy thing, full of knowing. He wasn't just playing; he was making sure Malren — and everyone else — knew exactly who held the reins in this room.

Malren, though, didn't flinch. Not an inch. That earned him a slow nod, as if The Knife respected that much at least.

Then, as if dismissing him entirely, The Knife

pivoted and strolled behind Finn and Pip, his presence shifting, a slow orbit around the two. His fingers drummed absently against Finn's shoulder, a gesture that might've seemed casual if not for the weight behind it. "We both know this isn't about justice. This is about who gives the orders and who pretends to follow them. And you—" he let his fingers press a little harder against Finn's collarbone "—you're just the poor bastard sent to collect."

He exhaled theatrically, shaking his head like a man beset by fools. "Well, far be it from me to get in the way of duty."

Pip caught the faintest shift—a flicker of motion at the edge of his vision, a subtle adjustment in stance—but realization came half a breath too slow.

The blackjack came down hard and fast, cracking against the base of his skull.

Pain split through his head—white-hot, sudden. His knees hit the floor first, the rest of him following, vision blurring at the edges. He tried to push up, to move, but his limbs were sluggish, unresponsive.

A sharp intake of breath—Darrik. A step forward, hesitation thick in his voice. "Boss—?" He hadn't seen it coming either. His shock cut through the room, an unspoken question hanging between them all.

The world buckled, tilted sideways—

And then—nothing.

## Chapter 21.    A Game Unraveling

---

The room smelled of untouched food. A tray sat on the small table near the bed, silver covers still fogged with the last of their warmth. The scent of roasted meat and stewed lentils thickened the air, mingling with the ever-present salt of the sea. Indaros sat in the chair beside it, boots propped against the edge of the table, spearing a bite of meat with the tip of his knife.

"You ordered it," he muttered around his mouthful. "I'm not letting it go to waste."

Aieria didn't answer. Behind the folding screen, she pulled the last strap tight around her thigh, securing the belt that held her climbing hooks. The snug fit of the leather against her limbs should have made her feel prepared, sharp, in control. It didn't.

She had failed.

She let out a slow breath, rolling her shoulders, testing the fit of her clothes. Lightweight, dark, built for movement—built for slipping unseen through the veins of the city. Her fingers lingered at the edges of the fabric, knuckles pressing against the ridges of her spine, the hidden scars beneath the cloth. The ghosts of wings that should have caught the wind, carried her over rooftops instead of leaving her scrambling up stone like a rat in the walls.

She pulled on her gloves, tightening the fingers as if that

would quiet the anger curling through her ribs.

"They ignored me."

Indaros swallowed, wiping his mouth on the back of his hand. "What?"

She stepped out from behind the screen, her jaw set. "I warned them. I told them exactly what was going to happen. And they ignored me."

Indaros didn't stop eating. He barely even glanced at her, just shook his head with a low, amused breath. "You really thought The Knife was going to listen to you?" He didn't say I told you so. He didn't have to.

She leveled a look at him, but he only jabbed his knife into another piece of meat. "Finn is innocent."

Indaros let out a laugh, dry and humorless. "No, he isn't."

Her fingers curled into fists at her sides. "The charges are false."

"He's a Butcher," Indaros said simply. "You know what they do for a living? Shakedowns. Murders. People disappear because of men like Finn. You call that innocent?"

She turned away, bracing her hands against the wooden frame of the open window. The night air curled against her skin, cool, weightless. "He doesn't deserve to be arrested for a crime he didn't commit."

Indaros shrugged, popping another bite into his mouth. "One less scumbag."

She squeezed her eyes shut. "That's not the point."

"Isn't it?" He finally looked at her, his gaze calm, steady. "You're getting worked up because you thought you had control of this. You thought you could move the pieces, play the game, and they just reminded you — you don't hold the board."

She grit her teeth, swallowing against the frustration that burned in her throat. He was right. And she hated it.

She exhaled sharply, forcing herself to think, to move. "Can I break him out?"

Indaros snorted. "No."

She barely hesitated. "Bribe the guards?"

"Not if the order came from Sargo himself. You'd need more gold than you have, and even then, no one's crossing The Duke over some slag."

Her fingers tightened around the windowsill. "Then he's already dead."

Indaros wiped his knife against his sleeve and leaned back in his chair. "Yep."

She turned to him sharply. "Then how do I make sure he doesn't die for nothing?"

Indaros sighed, rubbing a hand over his face. "This again."

"How do these trials go?" she pressed.

He didn't answer right away. For a moment, she thought

he might ignore her, but finally, he shook his head. "Charged. Guilty. Hanged. The end."

"That's it?"

"That's it." He rolled his shoulders. "People love it. A good hanging makes for a great show."

She turned back to the window, the wind teasing the edges of her hair. "Then we have to make it more. Make them feel the injustice."

Indaros snorted again. "Doesn't matter if the trial's fair or not. No one's expecting justice."

She set her jaw. "Fael will come through for me." The words left her lips, but she didn't believe them. Not really. Her grand plans, her careful maneuvering—just another dead end. Another lesson in folly.

Indaros didn't argue, but his silence spoke for him.

"The people will see the sham for what it is," she insisted, half to herself.

"They already know the courts are corrupt," Indaros said. "Don't care."

She let out a breath. She could feel the walls closing in, the weight of inevitability pressing down on her like a slow collapse. "How long do we have before the trial?"

Indaros leaned back in his chair, thinking. "Couple of weeks, maybe."

"Then Solivar better get to work."

She climbed onto the windowsill, adjusting the straps at her waist. Indaros watched her, unimpressed. "You know you can walk there, right?"

She glanced back at him, the faintest smirk ghosting across her lips. "I prefer this way. It clears my head."

And she needed that clarity now more than ever.

The city unfolded beneath her, a vast, tangled sprawl of rooftops and alleys, its veins pulsing with torchlight and shifting shadows. Aieria moved across the shingles, each step careful but fluid, her body finding the rhythm of the night. The air was thick with salt and distant smoke, the scent of the sea ever-present. Her fingers brushed against the rough stone of the ledge as she vaulted onto a lower roof, her boots barely making a sound.

She had never run like this before—not out of necessity, not for survival. Not when she had wings. The thought curled through her, unbidden. She had flown over cities, not through them. Had looked down from above, never tangled within their arteries. Now she had only muscle, balance, and breath.

She pressed forward, scaling a crumbling chimney, using it to propel herself to the next building, her breath measured, her heartbeat a steady drum against her ribs. She had thought she could control the game. Thought she could move the pieces, steer the fates of men with whispers and careful plays. But tonight had proven otherwise. She had warned The Knife, and he had ignored her. The city's rot ran too deep, its corruption so absolute that even the inevitable had become a spectacle. Justice was a performance here, its outcome never in question. She crouched at the edge of a slanted rooftop, staring down at the street below. Merchants haggled, thieves lurked in the dark pockets between buildings, the Watch moved in pairs, their armor dull beneath the street lanterns. The city pulsed, uncaring, unmovable.

She had fought for control, had believed she could carve out something of her own within Gatos. But tonight, she felt the weight of its indifference pressing down on her. Every move was blocked before she could even play it. Her breath came slow, measured, as she pushed forward again, running along the length of a wooden beam that connected two buildings. She leapt, landing with a soft thud against the stone of a bell tower, gripping the ledge before hauling herself up. The city stretched out before her, endless, impossible.

The whole city was rotten. The courts, the Watch, every system meant to keep order had already been bought and twisted into something unrecognizable. She had spent months studying, planning, learning the players and their weaknesses. She had thought she could wield that knowledge like a dagger. And now? Now, she was right where she had been before.

Powerless.

She had never felt so small.

She moved again, leaping onto the outer wall of the High Ward. The stone was cold beneath her hands, smooth in places where years of wind and rain had worn it down, rough in others where cracks had begun to form. It was an old wall, but still strong—like everything in the High Ward, built to last, to keep people like her out. She scaled it quickly, finding footholds with practiced ease, her body coiling and stretching in a rhythm that had become second nature. When she reached the top, she crouched, scanning the rooftops below. The High Ward was quieter than the rest of the city, its streets wide and orderly, its houses standing tall and proud, untouched by the filth that ruled the lower quarters.

Solivar's apartments lay ahead, nestled between two merchant estates. He had chosen well—his residence was neither ostentatious nor humble, but comfortably in between, allowing him to slip between worlds as easily as he spun his words.

She dropped down onto a balcony, rolling with the impact before rising smoothly to her feet. Her fingers found the edge of the window, testing the latch. Unlocked. Careless. Or perhaps intentional.

Slipping inside, she landed in a darkened sitting room. The air smelled of ink and old parchment, of wine left unfinished and candle wax melted down to its final flickers. Books and papers littered the space, strewn across tables and chairs in the way of a man who worked through inspiration rather than order.

Solivar.

Her lips pressed into a thin line. He was charming, talented, and too clever for his own good. And tonight, she was soured on him as well. She had put her faith in the wrong people—first The Knife, now him. She had thought she could move the Butchers, thought she could make them see reason. She had thought Solivar would be her weapon against the corruption of Gatos, that his words could shape the city as much as power and coin. But the more she studied this city, the more she understood the truth: it was not waiting to be saved. And

Solivar? He was not a weapon. He was an artist, a man who chased inspiration rather than justice. His loyalty was to his own legend, not to her cause.

But he was her last hope.

She exhaled slowly, steadying herself. She would not fail again. If Finn was doomed, if the courts could not be shaken, then she would make sure Gatos never forgot it. If she could not save a life, she could at least make sure his death meant something.

She moved deeper into the apartment, the scent of spilled wine growing thick in the air. A single candle flickered in the corner casting unsteady light over the room. Papers lay scattered across the floor, crumpled notes mingled with ink-stained napkins and half-empty bottles. A chair was overturned near the hearth, and on the couch, sprawled in the careless abandon of a man too drunk to care, lay Solivar.

His vest was unbuttoned, one sleeve half-rolled, the other still stiff with forgotten elegance. His usually neat curls hung loose and wild, falling over his eyes as he muttered something unintelligible into the space between wakefulness and oblivion. A near-empty goblet dangled from his fingers, its contents long since spilled onto the rug beneath him. He reeked of brandy and regret.

Aieria inhaled slowly, her patience thinning. This was what she had come to? This was the last thread of her plan? She had gambled on a poet drowning himself in his own indulgence.

She stepped forward, her boots deliberately loud against the wooden floor. "Solivar."

He groaned but did not lift his head. Instead, he waved a vague hand in her direction. "If you've come to kill me, at least let me finish the bottle first."

She crossed her arms. "Tempting. Get up."

He cracked one eye open, blinking blearily at her. "Ah. My dark and mysterious patron returns. How thrilling. Have you come to commission another grand work of rebellion? Or perhaps to scold me for my vices? I do so love when you play the righteous queen."

Aieria's jaw tightened. "I don't have time for this."

"Neither do I," he slurred, gesturing vaguely to the room around him. "The great bard is indisposed. Tragic, really. Gatos will have to live one night without my genius."

She moved swiftly, snatching the goblet from his fingers and tossing it aside, the metal clattering loudly against the floor. His gaze sharpened, if only slightly, as she loomed over him.

"You will listen to me."

For a moment, just a moment, something flickered in his gaze—something sober, something aware. Then it was gone, masked beneath the lazy smirk he wore so well.

"Always, my lady," he drawled. "Tell me, what desperate cause brings you to my humble den of misery?"

Aieria exhaled sharply, tamping down her frustration. "Chally Finn. The Butchers gave him up. He will stand trial in Gallows Square. A sham. A performance of justice. If it stands, he dies. And Gatos will cheer while it happens."

Solivar arched a brow, rubbing a hand over his face as if willing the alcohol to fade. "And you want me to do what? Sing him a ballad? Compose a mournful lament for a street thug?"

"I want you to turn him into something more than a street thug." Her voice was sharp, clipped. "I want you to make the people care. Make them see what this really is. You have power, Solivar. You move between the merchant courts and the gutters. People listen to you. And I need them to listen."

Solivar tilted his head, considering her. "You want sympathy. You want to make a Butcher into a tragic figure. I admire the ambition, but it's wasted."

She set her jaw. "Why?"

"Because people don't care about justice, Aieria. They care about entertainment." He rolled his shoulders, pushing himself upright, his eyes finally clearing. "A tragic figure? A man unfairly condemned? That might stir a handful of soft hearts, but the rest? They'll nod, sigh, and go back to their drink. No, if you want them to riot, to DEMAND his release, you have to give them something else. Not pity. Not righteousness. *Spectacle*."

Aieria frowned, but she let him continue.

"The people of Gatos love a show," he said, leaning forward. "That's what the trials are. That's why they're held in the square, why they're public hangings. You think they don't know it's a farce? They do. But they ENJOY it. If you want to turn them, you don't tell them the system is corrupt—they already know that. You make them laugh at it. You make it RIDICULOUS."

She was silent, absorbing his words. He saw it, smirked. "Make Finn a fool's martyr, not a noble one. Play the trial up as a game, a mockery. Turn it into something so obscene that even the lowest drunkard in the slums can't help but snicker. Let them laugh at their rulers, let them revel in the absurdity of it all. That's what will get under Bolter's skin. That's what will make Sargo's patience fray."

Aieria tapped her fingers against the back of a chair, the gears in her mind turning. "You think that will work."

"I think it's better than appealing to their moral compass." Solivar stretched, wincing slightly. "You want to stir the people? Give them a reason to laugh in Bolter's face. Make them feel powerful, even for a moment. That's what they crave."

She studied him, the exhaustion still lurking beneath his eyes, the sharp intelligence behind it. She hated that he was right. But she had no better plan.

She turned toward the window. "Then you'd best start writing."

Solivar chuckled, low and amused. "You know, most patrons request love songs."

As she stood there, watching Solivar gather his quill and ink, Aieria knew relying solely on a bard's words wasn't enough. It was time she stopped waiting for others to deliver results. "Tell your story, Solivar," she said quietly, turning towards the window, "and I'll tell mine. It's past time the city hears the truth — not just from you, but from me. I'll speak to Magistrate Fael directly and remind him of the consequences if justice falters."

He pushed himself to his feet in one fluid motion, stepping into her space, the sharpness in his eyes overtaking the bleariness of drink. "There are other ways to enjoy the night, you know." Before she could step back, he was close, one hand skimming over her hip, the other brushing the curve of her jaw. He moved like he belonged there, like the invitation had always been there waiting. And then, his lips caught hers.

For a breath, a single beat, she let him. Let him think he had won something.

Then she drove her knee into his ribs.

Solivar staggered back with a sharp grunt, one hand flying to his side. He let out a breathless laugh, half-pained, half-amused. "Dirty infighting? I like it."

Aieria wiped the back of her hand across her lips and smirked. "Then consider it a gift."

She vaulted onto the windowsill, turning back to watch him, still catching his breath, still grinning like he had gotten what he wanted anyway. She shook her head, pushing off into the night. As she moved across the rooftops, she realized, to her mild surprise, that she felt lighter. She had failed with The Knife. The trial was still a disaster waiting to happen. But, at least, something about what had just happened had lifted her spirits a little.

# Chapter 22.    The Visitor

"Don't get too close. He bit a man last week. Took a piece out of his cheek like a starving dog."

The jailer's voice was low, almost bored, but there was satisfaction in it too—the kind that came from telling stories meant to scare. His keys jingled at his side, a rhythm as constant as his steps down the spiraling stair.

Aieria didn't respond. Just nodded faintly, as though she hadn't heard him or had heard far worse.

Her borrowed dress was heavy and auburn-coloured, chosen to look expensive without drawing too much attention. The gloves were pale suede, near white, and too clean for the corridors they passed through. A shimmer clung to the hem of her cloak where torchlight caught it. Indaros walked behind her in a plain guard's cloak, one hand resting near the hilt of his blade, silent and watchful. He hadn't approved of this plan. He hadn't needed to say it.

When she'd told him, his silence had been louder than a shout. He'd looked at her like she was mad—and maybe she was. She'd built everything on caution, shadows, careful pressure behind closed doors. Now she was walking into one of the most watched, whispered-about cells in Gatos under a false name, flanked by a man who couldn't pretend not to care. The Red Knives would hear of this.

Someone might remember the shape of her face, the line of her voice, the dress. And once noticed, she couldn't be unnoticed again. The part of her that had learned to count costs already knew the truth: this was a gamble. A visible, foolish, emotional gamble. And if she lost, she wouldn't just lose him. She'd lose everything she'd clawed back from the ruin of who she used to be.

But still, she'd come.

She had told herself it was about control. About gathering leverage. About checking what opportunities might be developed to wrestle victory from disaster. But deep down, beneath all of it, was a simpler question: could she still save someone? Could she save herself?

She had taken the name Lady Merinthra of Oriven. A minor noble, quiet, charitable, deeply concerned with the plight of the accused. She wasn't the first woman to come. Gatos loved its monsters, and every monster drew its fair share of trembling do-gooders trying to wring redemption from blood. Most had been turned away. She had paid enough not to be.

The stairs gave way to a long, narrow corridor of damp stone. The air changed—thicker, close, and heavy with rot. Aieria caught the stink of human waste, old straw, and the slow, mildewed breath of walls that had been sweating for decades. The torches sputtered, weak flames clawing at a darkness that didn't want to leave.

They passed one cell, then another. The shapes inside barely stirred. Groans. Coughs. One pair of eyes tracked her, wide and glassy. Another face remained turned to the wall, unmoving. She felt each stare press against her skin like a bruise.

The jailer stopped at the final door, set apart from the others by rust and distance.

"You sure you want this? He hasn't said a word in days. Not anything that makes sense."

Aieria smiled, soft and unreadable. "Open it."

The jailer shrugged. He unlocked the gate with a metallic grunt, the iron hinges shrieking as the door gave way.

Indaros moved first, stepping into the dark with practiced caution. His blade stayed sheathed, but his posture shifted—ready, quiet, coiled. Aieria followed, slower, deliberate. She had not told him to stand aside, so he acted on instinct. That, too, was useful to her. Everyone played their part.

The cell was a mouth half-swallowed by dark. Low ceiling. Walls slick with moisture. A single barred window bled a shaft of weak light into the filth below. The floor was uneven stone, layered with damp straw and a dozen unspoken histories— bloodstains, old stains, streaks of something darker no one had bothered to scrub away. It reeked of old breath and rotted silence.

And there, in the corner, the thing they called Finn. He was barefoot, knees drawn to his chest, arms wrapped tight around them. His head was bowed, tangled hair hiding most of his face. What skin showed was mottled with bruises and grime. He didn't look up. Didn't move.

Aieria stood just inside the threshold, letting her eyes adjust. She had imagined madness. Rage. Maybe even defiance. What she saw instead was the kind of stillness that unnerved. This wasn't the posture of a man waiting to be saved. It was the posture of something left behind.

Indaros watched him in silence, tense but unreadable.

Aieria studied the shape in the straw. The body was gaunt. Starved. But not lifeless. Not yet. There was a charge in the air around him—a tension like a wire drawn too tight. Something that hadn't snapped. Not completely.

He shifted, slightly. Just enough to show that he was listening.

She took another step forward. Slowly, deliberately, she knelt. The straw whispered beneath her as her knees settled into it. She kept her back straight, her hands resting loosely on her thighs. Not reaching. Not pleading. Simply present.

"Finn," she said. Her voice was calm. Even.

Nothing. Not at first. Then slowly — painfully — his head turned. His eyes drifted past her at first, unfocused, hollow. Bleary. Bloodshot. For a moment, he looked through her, not at her — as if she were fog, or a dream he'd already forgotten. But something caught. There was a flicker in his gaze — recognition, or the ghost of it. As if she'd stepped into the wrong memory. Or the right one, out of order. His gaze sharpened, like a blade rusted at the edge but still able to cut.

Aieria met that gaze and didn't look away.

She wasn't sure what she'd expected, but it wasn't this. The man in this cell wasn't Chally Finn. Not unless Finn had somehow learned to shrink six inches, erase the weight in his shoulders, dull the gleam in his eye, and bury the venom in his voice. Everything she'd gathered — Indaros' description, the Watch reports, her own relentless overpreparation — had painted Chally Finn as tall, angry, reckless, coiled tight like a blade ready to bite. This boy was not that. Not remotely.

And she had met him before — not as Finn, but as something far more dangerous. The cheekbones were sharper now. The eyes dimmer. But they were the same. She didn't reach for him. Didn't speak. Just studied what was before her.

Pip.

The realization came cold. Like something slipping

down her spine.

The City Watch had arrested the wrong person.

For a heartbeat, Aieria almost felt relief. Because if it had truly been Pip — the Pip she remembered — then the noose might've been justice. Or at least survival. That boy had radiated death. Not the kind found in soldiers or hired killers, but something colder, older, something wrong. Letting him vanish into the dark of the gallows would have been... convenient.

Aieria's thoughts spiraled, trying to keep up with each other. Not only were the charges fabricated, the prisoner was the wrong man. Which meant that Sargo's orders were not followed. The blood debt would not be paid. The Knife *had* acted on her information, but to serve up Pip, not Finn. Why? That answer could wait. Justiciar Bolter would be revealed as completely incompetent. All the pieces might still fall into place. Her plan might work.

But it wouldn't feel like a victory.

Maybe there was a man god watching over this crazy city, playing all of them for its own crooked amusement. Because this boy — the one in front of her now, broken and near-mute — he was not the same creature who had stood behind Stone in the dark. *That* Pip had set her instincts howling, made her weigh every movement and every word like a knife. But this was not that. He wasn't a blade in the dark anymore. Just a dulled edge left to rust. A wreck that used to be a boy. A hollowed-out shape of a man with nothing at the centre. A boy too tired to lie, too broken to hide.

*Don't.*

It hit low—no grace to it, no warning. Just a punch from inside—sharp, unwelcome, unguarded. She knelt there in her borrowed name and borrowed clothes, built from lies and half-truths, and felt her eyes want to give. She wasn't supposed to feel this. Not anymore. Not after everything. She had watched cities fall. Had stood beneath severed banners while her wings bled out behind her. Nobility, grace—cut away in fire and ruin. She had reforged herself in the dark that followed, shaped her spine from ash and strategy, replaced instinct with calculation, mercy with silence. And still. God damn it, still. Some shard of the girl she'd been—the one who used to kneel beside the broken instead of stepping over them— rose up in her chest like rot through old stone. Whispering: not like this. Not him. Not now.

She hated that part. Hated that it had survived. Hated that it still moved inside her, twitching to life whenever she thought she'd buried it for good. It made her soft. Made her foolish. And worse, it made her remember what she used to believe—before the knives, before the silence, before the weight of the world made cruelty a kind of kindness. That girl had no place here.

But she was here all the same.

And then, from the straw and shadow, a voice rasped up.

"You came back."

It was barely a whisper, sanded raw by disuse and filth, but the words were clear.

Aieria froze. Not at the words, but the recognition folded inside them.

"I didn't," she said, before she could stop herself.

He made a sound—low, humourless. Might've been a laugh. Might've been the last breath of something that used to be hope.

"You remember me?" she asked.

He didn't nod. Didn't blink. Just said, "You named me."

The words hung in the air like smoke.

He was delusional. That much was obvious. Whatever damage had been done to him—by the streets, the cell, the life—it had blurred the lines in his head. She had never named him. Not really. And yet. Something about the way he said it tugged at her. Not just madness. Almost like somehow, in a way she only half understood, he wasn't wrong.

She heard herself speak before she meant to. "Are you hungry?"

He didn't lift his head. But he nodded.

And that was the worst of it. That she wanted to bring him food.

# Chapter 23.    Grinshard

The cell stank. Piss, mould, old sweat—layers thick enough to crawl into his nose and settle behind his eyes. Pip breathed through his mouth. It didn't help. The stink was in him now. Soaked through his skin. Made his stomach tighten, made his thoughts slow and foul. It reminded him of the Slag's back alleys—only here, there was no sky above, no wind to carry it off. It just sat with him. Twisted into his thoughts until he started wondering if the cell was inside him instead.

Pip didn't move much. The first few hours, maybe. Long enough to find the hard edges of the walls, count the rusted bolts in the door, test the strength of the hinges.

Time bent in a place like this. It stretched. Folded. Doubled back on itself. The sounds outside came in echoes—boots on stairs, keys in locks, the occasional sharp scream from farther down the corridor. There were other cells. Other poor bastards moaning through cracked lips, coughing into the straw, begging gods that never listened. Once, someone howled like an animal, full-throated and feral, until it cut off with a wet thud.

Pip didn't call out. Didn't scream. Didn't ask why.

He just lay there. Breathing. Thinking.

He thought about The Knife. The easy smile. The drink shared. The back of the head, turning away.

He thought about Darrik. That half-step forward. That hesitation. The look in his eyes when the blackjack came down. Not surprise. Not quite. Just disappointment. Like he'd known this was coming, and had hoped — stupidly — that it wouldn't.

Pip tasted blood again, thick in his mouth.

He lay in the filth, still as the stone beneath him. Not from pain. Not from the cut or the pounding in his skull. But because the air itself pressed him down, heavy with rot and memory. Moving meant thinking. Thinking meant remembering. And remembering hurt in ways the body didn't.

Part of him was missing.

He didn't feel it at first. Not really. He'd woken up cold and barefoot, half-dreaming, half-bleeding, jaw aching like someone had stepped on it. His boot was gone. Both boots. His knife, too. The bastard thing that whispered in his blood, that made killing easy. Gone.

For a while he thought maybe he'd hidden it too well. Maybe they'd missed it. Maybe he just couldn't feel it yet. But when he reached down and felt nothing there — just skin, bare and useless — it hit him like a wall. The Crooked Dagger was gone.

He didn't panic.

Not at first.

But hours passed. Or maybe days. The light in the window didn't change much, but he could tell. His thoughts frayed. Time crawled. He tried to sleep. Couldn't. Tried to speak. Nothing came.

Sometimes there were footsteps. Keys. A door clanging somewhere. A shout. Then silence again.

Always silence.

His thoughts pressed in, looping over old phrases, scraps of Darrik's voice and Slag-worn warnings. Not loud. Just small things. Phrases. Repeats. Things he'd heard once in the Slag. Things Darrik used to say.

*Never show the hand you mean to cut with.*

*Keep your mouth shut and your blade sharp.*

*Trust buys you a grave. Nothing more.*

He scraped those words into the stone with his fingernail until they bled. That helped some.

The cell got smaller. Or maybe his thoughts got bigger. He couldn't stop thinking about the dagger. About the feel of it. The cold curve. The way it swallowed him whole—mind, muscle, memory. Like it knew what he was before he did. The way it pulled. It was more than a weapon. It was part of him. And now it was gone. It was in someone else's hands. The thought didn't come all at once — it crept in slow, coiled like a sickness. At first, he denied it. Maybe it wasn't real. Maybe it was hidden, still his. But the truth settled in, cold and sharp. Someone had taken it. Someone was touching him. Someone holding him wrong. Touching him like he was just metal. They didn't understand. They thought he was just a knife. If they held him wrong, maybe he'd stop working. Maybe he'd cut them the way a lie cuts — quiet, deep, and all the way through.

The silence came back, thick and slow. The dark folded in behind it, swallowing what was left of time. He stared into it until it stared back — until it felt like it had eyes, breath, teeth.

Footsteps. Jingle. Clang. Light. A smell of food.

He tried to laugh. It came out wrong. Crooked. Like something had cracked behind his teeth.

The walls whispered to him.

They told their secrets. Whispers of the man who'd clawed his own eyes out after seven days with no light — said he saw his dead wife dancing in the corner, grinning with broken teeth. Of the preacher who'd stopped eating, said the cell fed him prayers — sweet, iron-rich verses he chewed like meat. And the boy. Gods, the boy. Said nothing. Not once. Just scratched tally marks into the wall with his teeth until he didn't have teeth anymore. The walls remembered them all. Carried the echo. Pressed their stories into Pip like rot into bone.

He whispered names to the dark—soft, broken things that meant nothing, until one of them stuck. It didn't come like a bolt. It seeped in, slow and certain. Familiar, though he couldn't say why. Like it had always been there, waiting.

And the dark said it back: *Grinshard.*

Not out loud—not really—but in that low way, the kind only the dark hears.

He was the dark. He'd crawled into a corner, slow and silent, like the rot itself. Like hiding from thought. Like becoming something else. Curled into the shape of himself. No—half of it.

He just had to remember the shape of himself.

But it was wrong now.

And the edges kept slipping.

And the darkness whispered back.

# Chapter 24.    A Stage Fit for a King

The city was alive.

Gatos had seen its share of spectacle—duels of honour fought in high courts, blood spilled in dark alleys, ships set ablaze in the harbour while the desperate leapt screaming into the sea. But this was something else. This was theatre on a scale so grand that even the walls of the Gallows Square struggled to contain it.

And who, pray tell, had made it so?

Solivar smiled to himself, leaning against the second-floor balcony of The Gilded Parrot, an establishment of some refinement (by Gatos standards), where the scent of perfumed oils clashed with the stale musk of too many bodies packed too close. Velvet curtains framed the arched entryways, their deep burgundy folds concealing whispered dealings and languid embraces in the private lounges beyond. A silver tray rested at his elbow, bearing a half-finished carafe of sparkling Merovan red, refilled the moment it dared to dip below half-full by a dark-eyed serving girl whose attentions were as professional as they were playful.

"You do enjoy watching them, don't you?" she murmured, placing a fresh carafe on the tray with a knowing smile. Solivar tilted his head toward her, amused.

"Nothing like a captive audience," he remarked dryly, eyes glittering with quiet satisfaction.

The energy rippled through the crowd, an intoxicating current beneath the surface, one that he alone had stirred. It was a delicate thing, this power — not the blunt force of steel or coin, but something far finer. Words, spun like silk, threaded through the fabric of the city until they wove a tapestry so vivid that no one questioned its authenticity. It was his song they moved to, his unseen hand shaping the rhythm. And now, as the city trembled on the edge of revelation, he savoured the moment, luxuriating in the knowledge that none of them, not a single one, understood how thoroughly they danced to his design.

The ground was packed earth, churned into thick mud where the morning's refuse had mixed with the trampling of a thousand restless feet. Ragged beggars crouched at the fringes, hands outstretched for coin or crust, their hollow eyes drinking in the pageantry. Vendors called out from their stalls, hawking honeyed dates, sizzling eel skewers, and flasks of bitter juniper gin, their voices near drowned by the constant roar of the gathering crowd.

Buildings of varying prestige framed the square like silent spectators, their weathered facades coated in a fine layer of city grime. To the east, the Copper Guild Exchange loomed, its high iron gates shut tight, as if the merchants inside wished to deny their proximity to such vulgar proceedings. The Broken Maiden, a gaming house and brothel draped in red lanterns, had thrown open its balconies, its girls lounging lazily, tossing apple peels and calling wagers on whether the condemned would cry for mercy.

And at the heart of it all, the gallows stood waiting.

A simple thing — wood, rope, a single step between life and death. The frame had been newly scrubbed, its boards bleached under the sun, though no effort could erase the deep grooves in the planks where so many had kicked and thrashed in their final moments. The noose swung gently in the wind, a silent reminder that for all the revelry, the city had gathered to watch a man die.

The lords and ladies, their silks and velvets shimmering in the light, occupied the raised platform to the west, shaded beneath a billowing crimson canopy. Some held lace-edged handkerchiefs to their noses, as if offended by the scent of common flesh. Here, beneath rich silks, sat the architects of Gatos' power — Duke Sargo himself, draped in embroidered crimson, his heavy-lidded eyes betraying only mild interest; beside him, Lord Edran Bolter, Grand Judiciar of the city, his mouth set in a line of grim satisfaction, as though watching justice play out by his own divine hand. Lady Valcora Drevis, draped in layers of pearls, fanned herself languidly, the only sign of her excitement the slight flush creeping up her powdered cheeks.

Below them, the merchants and tradesmen stood shoulder to shoulder, their wealth measured not in titles but in the quality of their boots and the weight of the rings on their fingers. Lesser nobles, those without the means to buy a seat among the true elite, mingled with them, muttering complaints of exclusion while ensuring their fine gloves did not brush against coarser fabrics.

And beyond them, packed so tight there was barely room to breathe, the city's poor surged like a restless tide — dockhands, pickpockets, sellswords, and street urchins, all drawn by the promise of justice or vengeance, depending on whom you asked. They would see no justice here, of course—only the illusion of it, handed down from men who had never known hunger. But illusion had always been enough to pacify the masses, so long as it was played convincingly.

The City Watch was out in full force, polished steel glinting in the sun, their Marshal perched near the gallows with the stiff-backed bearing of a man who knew this day could turn against him in an instant. Their presence was both a deterrent and a provocation—after all, nothing made a mob thirstier for blood than the sight of men sworn to keep them in check.

And above it all, dangling stemware between careless fingers, Solivar watched.

From his balcony of the Gilded Parrot, he had the finest seat in the city. The wind tugged at his sleeves, carrying the mingled cacophony of the square upward—the shouted wagers, the drunken laughter, the occasional jeer aimed at the gallows.

The girl refilled his cup, lingering just long enough to be an invitation. "Enjoying the show?" she asked, her voice a careful balance of curiosity and flirtation.

Solivar let his gaze trail over her, drinking in the smooth expanse of sun-bronzed skin, the subtle curve of her collarbone disappearing beneath the crisp white of her bodice. The neckline plunged just enough to suggest, to invite, without offering outright surrender—an artist's restraint in the game of temptation. Her lips, full and wickedly upturned, carried the remnants of a smirk, the kind a woman wore when she knew exactly how much power she held.

"Immensely," Solivar murmured at last, turning the goblet in his fingers, watching the way the deep red liquid fractured the light. "Though I fear the ending may be disappointingly predictable."

She tilted her head, feigning innocence. "And what ending would you prefer?"

He smiled, letting the silence stretch between them just long enough to be deliberate.

"One with just enough tragedy to be mistaken for truth," he said. "And just enough triumph to keep them coming back for more."

Below, the city pulsed with expectation. This moment, this grand theatre of justice and retribution, was not the work of kings or lords.

It was words.

His words.

He had set this in motion. He had fanned the flames, turned whispers into songs, speculation into certainty, doubt into fervour. A trial, yes—but what was a trial without an audience? A dreary thing, a bureaucratic footnote. But with the right voice, the right turn of phrase, a little poetry slipped between the cracks of daily life?

Well. That was how you built a legend.

Chally Finn was no one. A Butcher, a petty thug turned unfortunate scapegoat, handed over by his own kind for reasons that didn't matter. No one had cared when he was shackled. No one had cared when a Lower Court judge, with all the solemnity of a clerk tallying turnips, signed off on his fate—though, of High Judiciar Bolter's hand had been guiding the pen from the shadows.

But they cared now, didn't they?

Justice in Gatos was a blunt instrument, a cudgel dressed in silk. No one believed in its purity, but everyone enjoyed watching it swing. So Solivar had given them something to watch.

It had begun in the way all great performances did: with an opening line worth remembering.

"Hear about this public trial?" Solivar announced from the stage, his voice carrying effortlessly over the gathered nobles, his goblet held aloft as if toasting the absurdity of it all. The candlelight caught the glint in his eye, a flicker of mischief, of calculation. "Poor bastard hasn't even been sentenced yet, but they've already measured his rope."

The words spread. From the stage to the nobles, from the nobles to their high servants, from high servants to low ones, until the echoes of Solivar's performance dripped down through the layers of the city like spilt wine soaking into linen. A Lady's laughter over dinner became a whispered retelling between chambermaids. A passing jest in a merchant's hall turned into a drunken boast by his coachman. The kitchens hummed with it, the laundresses gossiped over sudsy basins, and by the time the words reached the streets, they had been polished and reshaped into something even sharper, even more absurd. The wine hall murmured. The docks grumbled. The betting dens sharpened their knives. Because, really—what fun was an execution without the thrill of a wager?

And then the questions began.

What had Finn done to deserve such expediency? How had a commoner commanded such attention? What whispered scandal, what unseen blunder had made him the subject of so many careful conversations?

These questions received answers, each more fantastical than the last. A high lady had taken Finn to her bed, they whispered, and her husband had demanded his head for the insult. No—he had been caught with not one, but two noblewomen, and the judges were merely covering up the scandal. A merchant swore he had heard from a friend of a friend that Finn had stolen a relic, something precious, something dangerous. A book, a dagger, a key to a vault deep below the city, where ancient things slumbered. A courtesan in the High Ward insisted he was ravishingly handsome, his list of noble conquests so long that scandal had turned to bloodshed. The women, mad with jealousy, had begun feuding over him in secret, each unwilling to let another possess what they could not claim entirely. Some said they had resolved to have him chopped into pieces and shared among them, a grotesque pact of devotion and spite. Finn was no mere criminal— he was, in fact, a long-lost prince, the bastard son of an exiled king who had been hiding among the Butchers until the courts had caught wind of his birthright. The trial, they said, was not about justice but about silencing a rightful heir before he could reclaim his throne. He had been smuggled into Gatos as a babe inside a merchant's wine barrel, raised in secrecy by a blind swordsman who had taught him to fight with uncanny precision. Finn had bested Sargo himself in a masked duel at a noble's private gathering, slicing a button clean from the Duke's embroidered vest.

But Solivar's favourite, the one that nearly had him choking on his wine, was this: Finn was no mere man at all, but a trickster god in disguise, walking among mortals to test their wit and worth. And oh, how they had failed him. This was no trial, no execution—it was a divine jest, and when the noose tightened around his neck, he would simply vanish in a puff of golden smoke, reappearing in some distant land to drink and gamble and mock the foolishness of men. The priests, naturally, scoffed at this. But they scoffed a little too loudly, and some began to wonder if they feared it might actually be true.

By the time Solivar had overheard a group of dockworkers arguing—heatedly—about whether Finn was truly the chosen hero prophesied to free the city from tyranny, he knew his work was complete. What was truth, after all, but a story well told?

Better still: did it even matter? In the end, no one was entirely sure what he had done. Only that it must have been *something*. Because why else would the city be so obsessed?

Justice should be swift, they said. A clean cut. Efficient. That was how these things were handled.

And yet.

The trial should have arrived within days. Instead, scheduling stretched to a week. Then two. Then three. Oh, but the courts were so full, weren't they? A merchant dispute in the High Ward had pushed the docket. The city watch had concerns—public interest, you see, too many eyes, too much unrest, best to schedule more guards, more control.

Bolter seethed.

Sargo fumed.

Solivar poured another drink and watched it unfold like the inevitable second act of a play only he had read.

"This was supposed to be done," Sargo snarled one evening, pacing the halls of his gilded prison, his so-called palace—the Gilded Warden's seat, as the people called it. "Bolter, do you hear me? I wanted this finished."

Bolter heard him, all right. Heard him and festered, cold and rigid as the marble beneath his feet, his fury leaking out in clipped commands, in the grind of his jaw, in the way his carefully ordered system was collapsing under the weight of its own absurdity.

They had wanted a hanging. A quiet one.

The blind, the mad, the drunk—Gatos' insatiable horde—demanded spectacle, not justice. Solivar's silvered tongue wove itself through the city, unspooling Bolter's careful noose one meticulous, thrumming thread at a time, until the execution was no longer a necessity, but a legend in the making.

The more time he had, the more he wove. A song here, a murmured joke there, a suggestion in a wine-drunk ear that perhaps, just perhaps, this wasn't justice at all but comedy. Finn the Fool, Finn the Doomed, Finn who would hang before his trial had even begun.

And oh, how they laughed.

By the time the date of the trial was announced, the city

was no longer angry. The city was invested. The brothels had placed bets. The nobles had picked favourites. The streets hummed with anticipation.

Bolter had lost control.

The more Bolter pushed, the more the city dragged its feet. The courts stalled, the guards hesitated, the papers vanished, the ink smudged, the right official conveniently bedridden. No one was working anymore—they were talking, arguing, laughing, wagering. The city had ceased its daily grind and turned, as one, toward the spectacle unfurling before them. It was no longer just an execution; it was an event, a shared obsession, a stage upon which the entire city now stood.

And then, oh, then Sargo changed his tune.

"I suppose," he murmured one evening, fingers tapping against a goblet of wine, "there's money to be made in all this."

An obsessed populace was a happy, diverted populace. Coin flowed; spirits soared. More pockets were picked in the frenzy, more wagers placed, ensuring the house always won more. Merchants flooded the streets, hawking wares to a city too enthralled to count its coin with care.

And that was that. The trial wasn't a nuisance anymore. It was an investment.

The square needed to be expanded. More guards. More spectacle. More of everything. The gallows had to be reinforced; the platform widened. A scaffold fit for a king, fit for a spectacle, fit for a man who had become a story before the noose had ever touched his neck.

Solivar leaned against the balcony, swirling his wine as the city thrummed below.

"You wanted them to care," he murmured to Aieria, as if she were there beside him, lips curled in that knowing way, sky-blue eyes gleaming with appreciation. "But caring is dull, my dear. It has limits. What they feel now?" He swirled his wine, watching the city pulse with anticipation below. "This is better."

# Chapter 25.    The Gallows Masquerade

She had always thought the world would end with silence.

Instead, it began with a crowd.

Thousands packed into the square, clinging to ledges and balconies, swarming over every step and stone. Above them, the sky was endless blue—too clean, too bright. A brisk wind snapped banners and tugged at cloaks, carrying laughter, shouts, and the scent of dust. The gallows loomed above it all, tall and absurd. Not justice. Not punishment. Performance.

Aieria stood veiled in the magistrate's pavilion, high above the square, the stone beneath her feet warm from the morning sun. The wind tugged at the hem of her borrowed gown, snapping her veil against her cheek in sharp little flicks. Her position offered her a perfect view—of the gallows, the mob, the twisting chaos of movement and sound below—but she couldn't seem to see any of it clearly. The light was too bright. The air too clean.

Her fingers twitched beneath the silk. Not fear. Not yet. Something worse. Something she refused to name. But it stirred in her chest, unwelcome and old. The shape of something she'd buried long ago clawing its way back to the surface.

Recognition.

Because this was what she'd built—brick by brick, lie by lie. She had pushed the wheel. And now it turned.

The court moved around her—words, verdicts, speeches from mouths that meant nothing. Fael sat like a man still hoping to wake up. Aieria watched him from across the pavilion, her expression unreadable beneath the veil. She had spoken to him last night, in a chamber too quiet and too dim, when the city had already begun sharpening its knives. She had pleaded—subtly, carefully, but pleaded all the same. And Fael, in that weary voice of his, had said he'd done all he could. That the trial would be fair. That they'd have to see.

He was seeing it now.

She could see the sweat soaking through his collar, his fingers clutching the scrolls like they could anchor him. He wore full regalia, perfect to the last button—as if ceremony might make the theatre real. But he looked small. Smaller than she'd ever seen him. A man wrapped in symbols that no longer mattered. And she hated that she'd hoped, even for a moment, that he would resist. That he would stand for something.

The scrolls in his lap fluttered in the wind, unread and useless. He gripped them anyway, as if they might still matter. As if words had weight in a place like this.

Aieria's gaze passed over that Butcher, Stone—burly, stone-faced, and unremarkable, his expression giving away little. Still, even from a distance, she caught something in the weariness of his posture, the bitterness in the tightness of his jaw. He appeared disillusioned, resigned—a pragmatic man standing silent amid the spectacle.

Solivar leaned forward from the second-floor balcony of The Gilded Parrot, one elbow propped on the railing, his pen already dancing across parchment. The tavern had thrown open its shutters to sell overpriced wine and a view of the gallows, and Solivar had claimed the best seat in the house. He sipped from a glass of something sparkling and unnecessary, grinning as though he were reviewing a play.

Aieria felt something twist. She had asked him for this—his words, his talent, his knack for slipping stories into the public throat like a knife between ribs. He had delivered, as always. Charm and scandal, ink and myth. He'd made the trial matter. Made it sing. And now here he was, watching it play out with a drink in one hand and delight in his eyes, like she hadn't meant for the cut to land where it did—too deep, through the bone. Like she wasn't standing in the middle of a fire she had begged him to help light. Every scream, every cheer, every flicker of motion below—fodder for the ballad already forming in his head.

The noble pavilion rose on the west side of the

square, draped in silks and striped banners, a patch of calm above the chaos. Raised high enough for comfort but not so high as to miss the execution, it held polished chairs and shaded tables, silver trays with sweating wine bottles, a string quartet poised like props just behind the curtain. She had never set foot inside it. Never been invited. And standing here now, on stone and grit, she didn't want to. It stank of power trying too hard not to look afraid.

Three men sat at its centre.

One, broad-shouldered and scarred, leaned forward like he was waiting for something he'd paid for. Dressed in a tailored coat that fit too well to be honest, he didn't sip from the silver goblet beside him. Didn't speak. Just watched with a stillness that suggested something deeply personal. Aieria didn't know his name. Didn't need to. Men like him didn't chase justice. They paid to see a body fall.

Beside him sat Sargo, unofficial King of Gatos, the rot in his belly hidden by red velvet and gold thread. His face was drawn, not from concern but from heat and boredom. He looked like a man who wanted the afternoon to be over, who hated being reminded that the mob existed.

Next to him—Bolter. She had never seen him in the flesh, only studied the angles of his face in sketches, read the quiet notes written in a dozen coded hands. But she knew it was him the moment he turned to whisper. Narrow-eyed, pale-skinned, mouth set like a trap. He was smaller than she'd imagined. Less imposing. But the chill that ran through her when their eyes nearly met was all too real.

She looked away. Quickly. They didn't matter. Not anymore. Not here. Not now.

The square churned like a living thing — hot, restless, packed tight as pressure in a sealed room. From above, they looked almost beautiful: a field of colour and motion. But the voices told a different story — rising, folding, tense. Hungry. Vendors barked. Children climbed. Old men shoved. Too many people. Too much heat. One spark, and it would all go. She knew that, even before the sentence was read. Even before the rope was tightened. The city had been waiting for a reason. And today, it had one.

Time seemed to pause — not with grace, but with tension stretched to its thinnest thread.

Aieria looked at the crowd, the platform above the city like an altar waiting for blood. The breeze ruffled hair and banners, and for one sharp, crystalline moment, she thought: It won't hold. None of this will hold.

The air smelled of dust and smoke and anticipation.

And then —

The thread snapped.

The guards led him out.

Chains on his wrists. Sack over his head. Shirt clinging to his frame with dried blood and sweat. He stumbled once on the uneven boards of the gallows ramp, and one of the guards jerked him upright like a dog on a chain. He looked smaller than she remembered. Smaller than anyone should've been. They made him stand. Centre stage. The wind caught the hem of his tunic and fluttered it like a torn flag. Then the hood was pulled away.

Pip squinted in the light. Blinked like a man waking up from somewhere very far away. And for a moment—just a heartbeat—he turned his face upward, toward the sun.

Aieria felt her stomach drop.

Not because he looked at her. He didn't. But because in that moment, she saw the boy—not the monster, not the mistake, not the weapon or the myth. Just a boy. One too thin to stand straight. One who should never have been here.

The Master's voice rang out, flat and rehearsed.

"Chally Finn, accused of murder, conspiracy, and unlawful interference with the Watch. How do you plead?"

The lawyer beside him—a man who hadn't spoken a word to Pip—stood up and said, "Guilty."

Aieria felt her mouth open before she could stop it. She nearly stepped forward. Nearly screamed.

*His name is Pip! Pipfinzinder! Not Finn. Not this lie. Not this farce.*

But she didn't move. Couldn't. She could only watch in horror as the gavel struck wood and the crowd surged.

Her eyes flicked to Fael. His lips parted, slow with disbelief. His hands dropped the scrolls without realizing. He turned to the Master beside him — but the man was already looking away, already finished.

*Where is your justice now?* she thought. But it was not a question. It was a requiem.

It wasn't a trial. It had never been. It was a stage. A sentence. A clean line drawn through a life.

Across the pavilion, Sargo squinted. He shifted in his seat, leaned toward Bolter, said something too low to carry. But his body said it all. Irritation sharpened to confusion. Then disbelief. His hand sliced sideways through the air — a gesture that didn't need words.

*What the hells is this?* he seemed to say. *That's not Finn.*

Bolter's face didn't move. Not at first. Then his lips pressed thin. He answered with a single shake of his head. Whether it meant no, or not here, or too late — Aieria couldn't tell. But the crack had formed. She saw it. A sliver of doubt where certainty used to live.

And the boy still stood there, swaying in the wind,

waiting to die.

The guards moved again—rough hands on his arms, marching him the last few steps to the gallows post. One of them adjusted the rope. The other placed the noose over his head with mechanical ease, like stringing up a sack of grain.

The crowd grew louder.

Aieria could feel it. The swell. The pitch. The mood turning not toward silence, but noise. Roaring, restless noise. The kind that came before a break.

The Watch had formed a ring around the gallows, cudgels out, shields raised, already pushing back the front ranks. Someone shouted. Someone else screamed. The sound wasn't words anymore. It was pressure.

A functionary in court robes stepped forward with a scroll, hands trembling more with each step. He was young—too young for this post—and sweat clung to his hairline despite the breeze. He broke the seal clumsily, fingers fumbling the wax, casting nervous glances at the roaring mass below. The noise had turned. Louder. Meaner. A tide rising against the walls. He unrolled the scroll with too much flourish, perhaps thinking it might lend him dignity. Then he began to speak.

No one heard him.

The crowd surged forward, pressing against the

barricades, shouting, screaming, jeering. Justice, vengeance, spectacle — whatever they'd come for, it was no longer orderly. The Watch braced themselves, shoving, swinging, snarling warnings into the press. The functionary's voice rose, cracking with panic. Still nothing. The wind carried his words away, shredded them, tossed them into the sky.

He kept reading, as if the words might shield him.

No one heard a word.

The crowd was too loud. The square too tight. The wind snapped his words away before they landed.

And then —

It started as a flash of glass — thrown from the crowd — sparkling in the sun. A bottle, alight and spinning, crashing against the foot of the scaffold. Flames curled up the wood like they'd been waiting, dry boards and tar-stained rope drinking it deep.

The sky winked.

A moment of silence suddenly descended. Two thousand eyes watched as fire erupted on the gallows.

And then--

A shriek of burning flesh tore it apart.

The functionary recoiled, his robes licking orange.

He turned to run—but the silk went up like parchment. He vanished in a burst of fire and smoke, screaming, arms pinwheeling as he stumbled off the platform. Somewhere in the mob, someone laughed.

The gallows cracked like dry bone. The crowd surged. The front ranks broke, the Watch trying to hold them with cudgels and shouts—but they were swallowed, dragged into the riot like stones in a flood. Shields vanished beneath bodies. One soldier disappeared screaming beneath the boots of the mob.

Fire raced up the scaffold, then leapt. A flaming beam tumbled into the barricades. A merchant cart exploded in sparks and sugar. Hot oil sprayed a wall of men who'd been selling pies two minutes earlier. Now they ran, faces peeling, shrieking as they slapped at their melting skin.

The wind carried the fire like a lover.

The Gilded Parrot's balcony cracked and collapsed, spilling rich fools into the fire they'd paid to witness. One woman hit the stones headfirst, another flailed into flame with her skirts lit. Solivar's chair was empty—parchment fluttering, half-written verse burning line by line.

Then the nobles pavilion caught.

Banners curled black. Velvet burst into flame with a hiss and roar. Aieria saw a nobleman trip trying to drag his wine-soaked mistress away—only for the structure to come down on both of them. One of the musicians was still playing, violin howling through the fire like some mad prayer, until a falling pole drove through his chest and pinned him to the stage.

Bolter was gone.

Sargo burned.

The scarred man simply stood there, watching.

The fire leapt again. Awnings and rooftops. A row of apartments cracked like kindling. Smoke towered, thick as ink. A pack of fleeing watchmen slammed into a fruit cart and were buried in fire and apples. One clawed his way out, screaming until his voice melted.

And in the centre, Pip.

The flames curled around him. The noose still hung loose from his neck, swaying with the wind. His eyes were wide and far away, reflecting the blaze like gold. Ash drifted around him, clinging to his shoulders like a cloak. He did not move. The gallows burned beneath his feet. The rope snapped. And still he stood. Untouched. Unharmed. Eyes glowing with something not entirely sane. Like a trickster god watching the world burn just to see what would crawl out of the ashes.

The fire surged into the Low Ward like floodwater—ravenous and directionless. It didn't spread so much as consume, devouring tenements, alleys, anything soft enough to burn. Doors burst inward. Windows shattered. Flames climbed like breath caught too long—eager, alive, tasting the wood as if it were flesh. It caught tenements and trash heaps and the bones of buildings too old to stand. Screams blurred together into a single wild animal sound. Horses trampled children. Mothers stabbed strangers to clear a path.

And still the fire climbed.

Past the markets. Past the shrines. Up against the stone wall of the High Ward—the last, proud barrier between old money and the rest of Gatos. But pride wasn't fireproof. The wind lifted the flames high, hurling them over the wall in great arcs of burning cloth and shattered timber.

It reached over the gates. Into the gardens. Through the carved doors and mirrored halls. Into marble villas and silken beds. Nobles tried to flee with silver in their hands and smoke in their throats. Some wept. Some begged. Some simply ran until they collapsed in flames.

Smoke poured from every window like the city itself had become a forge.

Nothing was safe.

No one knew where to run.

The air boiled.

And in the middle of it all, Pip just watched.

Smiling.

Then the fire reached the base of the magistrate's pavilion. Indaros pulled her away, and the last thing she saw was the square devouring itself.

The fire had gutted Gallows Square, but Gatos did not stop burning. Not really. It smouldered now — beneath stone, behind doors, inside men who refused to grieve. The Gallows still stood, somehow. Blackened. Tilted slightly east like it knew it was finished but hadn't been told.

Stone passed it each morning. Didn't look at it. Not really. He just noted the absence of the crowds, the quiet, the stink of ash buried under piss and old rot. Life, such as it was, had returned to the city. Or pretended to.

The Low Ward had burned deepest. Stone and timber baked to ruin; whole blocks scorched to bone. The court still stood, and the jail, though both bore the scars — walls blackened, iron warped, the scent of charcoal soaked into every hinge. What passed for justice in Gatos now smelled like a ruined hearth.

The High Ward escaped with its pride half-intact. The fires had touched it, yes, but only lightly. A few towers, a few galleries. All the pretty things. Sargo's mansion had lost half its front, the stone now a melted, pitted thing that looked more like a jawbone than a home. He'd taken to meeting in the inner parlour now, curtains drawn. No one spoke of it aloud, but the image lingered.

The Docks had taken it hard. Wood and canvas and

pitch, all perfectly arranged for ruin. The fire had gutted it like a belly opened too fast. Rat-Eye had vanished before it came, or maybe during. No one knew. The wind had been blowing uphill—mercifully, if you could call it that. If it hadn't, the whole waterfront would be nothing but cinders and fishbone.

The Slag had burned worst of all.

It was always going to. Wood stacked over wood, hovels built on rot, everything held together by memory and mould. A firepit pretending to be a neighbourhood. When it went up, it went fast. Whole families swallowed in minutes. No screams made it past the first hour. The ground, silt-heavy and wet in its bones, eventually fought back. The fire hit mud and steam, and the city choked on the result. When it cleared, the Slag was gone. Just black sticks in muck, like ribs of something long-dead.

They were back to collections now. Fistwork. Threats. Rotgut coin from lean-faced men who barely had enough to cover bread. One mark pissed himself when Stone showed up. Another offered his daughter. Stone took the coin, left the rest. That passed for honour these days.

The Butchers were barely a dozen now. Shadows of shadows. Most had fled. A few had died fighting over scraps. The rest had turned silent, watchful, afraid of their own knives. No one said it, but everyone knew: the Butchers were dead. They just hadn't been buried yet.

Sargo had moved The Knife to the Docks. What was left of them, anyway. Rat-Eye was gone. The Slag had turned to charcoal. The Knife knew nothing about cargo or tide tables or tariffs, but he held the Crooked Dagger, and no one dared say otherwise. The crews were a stitched-together mess now — dock thugs, Wharfdogs, Low Dogs, whatever scraps of Butchers remained. The name didn't matter anymore.

The Knife still held court. If you could call it that. No loyal fists, no solid crew — just stragglers and scraps around a burned-out table. He kept sharpening blades that didn't need it. Same strokes, same muttering. Low. Sour. The man had become a habit wrapped in skin. He looked thinner now. Not starving — just hollowed out. Pale around the mouth. Eyes like he'd forgotten how to blink. Still dangerous, in that cornered way. A rat with a name and a weapon, and nothing to lose. He never asked for loyalty anymore. Just expected it. Like gravity. Or rust.

Stone gave it. Out of habit. Out of caution. Out of the simple fact that someone had to.

He ran the jobs. Kept the dock crews from tearing each other apart. Bargained bribes with men too broke to pretend at law. There wasn't much left to hold together, but what there was, he held.

Stone worked. Thought about Pip more than he should.

Not the fire. Not the gallows. That was a blur—flame and shouting and something hollow underneath. No, he thought about before. The boy's eyes when he worked. The way he held the dagger like it belonged to him and no one else ever had a claim.

And the betrayal. It came like a trick of routine. No flare, no announcement. One command, one look, and suddenly Pip was on the floor with blood in his hair.

The Butchers' Guildhouse. Wasn't much. Never had been. Wood and stone, drafty in winter, leaky in the rains. But it was theirs. Meant something, once. You fought for it. Bled into the cracks. Shared drink at the end of bad nights. Not home, but close enough.

Now the Watch were inside. Moving slow, measured, like they didn't want to admit they'd already won. Malren stood at the front, posture loose, eyes already past it. Like he'd come to sweep up and didn't care what broke along the way.

The Knife moved slow, like he wanted people to think he wasn't watching. Like he was just passing time, instead of steering it.

"Well, far be it from me to get in the way of duty," he said. Calm. Hands up like he was being helpful. Like it was all routine. Stone had seen that look before—right before something broke.

Then the blow came. Blackjack to the skull. Fast. Efficient. No drama. Pip dropped like a snuffed candle. A wet thump and then stillness. Tried to move, for a heartbeat. Tried to lift his head. Didn't matter.

Stone stepped forward. "Boss—?" Just the one word. Came out dry. He hadn't planned to say it. It was habit, reflex. But that didn't matter. Pip heard it. That was enough. Enough to make it feel the betrayal. The boy's eyes had opened just long enough to understand.

The Knife crouched. Went through Pip's coat like a man checking for broken glass. Hands twitchy, but focused. Careful, like he half-expected the boy to wake and take his throat. Then he found it—the Crooked Dagger. Drew it from the sheath like it might come alive in his hand. Then he wrapped it tight in cloth, fast and neat. Clutched it like it could keep him warm through the winter.

"This is Finn," he said, standing up straight. Suddenly sure again. "Figured we didn't need a scene."

They hauled Pip up. Dragged him away like cargo. Stone said nothing. Couldn't. His mouth had turned to brick. His hands felt nailed to his sides.

He drank more. Slept less. Worked harder. Still carrying what was left of it. Debt, blood, and bad choices. Some nights, he went back to the old corner.

Where they used to sit. Dice scars still in the wood. His cup. Pip's silence. That had meant something. Not friendship. Recognition.

Now there was only Stone. Still breathing, still showing up. A crew behind him, sure—but they weren't Butchers. Not really. Not yet. Just muscle with names. It didn't matter. Someone had to keep things upright. If he didn't, no one would. And maybe that was true. Maybe not.

The Crooked Dagger rode The Knife's hip now. Cracked leather. Always within reach. Pretending the blade made him matter.

One morning, Stone would stop pretending it meant anything.

Today, he just pulled on his gloves.

Back to work.

---

They found Sorren in what passed for a den—half a basement under the burnt-out shell of a warehouse. The fire had taken the rest. This part clung on. Wet, scorched, barely upright. Still breathing, though. Gatos had plenty of places like that.

Ceiling weeping. Stone sweating through the walls. Smell of smoke, grease, sweat. Sorren had rebuilt with leftovers. Bent chairs. Cracked tables. Cards slapped against scorched planks. Every third man had a blade. Every second owed someone.

Stone didn't say a word walking in. Just let his boots do the talking. Crew filled in behind him, tight and steady.

Hookhand came first. Built for trouble. That hook of his scraped metal, and the room got quieter. Lantern kept to the back. Didn't need much space to watch everything. Fingers already moving in the old code. No ships. No eyes. Seasnake leaned on the far wall. Arms crossed. Waiting. She didn't need to speak. She never did.

Sorren tried for casual. Came out shaky. "Just a misunderstanding, boys. Coin's moving slow these days—"

Stone stepped forward. Slow. Pulled the ledger from inside his coat.

"Sixty-seven crowns skimmed. Lied about thirty-nine. Nothing paid back."

Didn't raise his voice. Didn't need to. The numbers spoke fine on their own.

Sorren looked around. No help coming. Just the steady drip of water and the hook waiting to swing.

"You want it back?" he asked, voice barely there.

Stone shook his head. "No."

Hookhand moved like a man folding laundry. Two cracks, clean and final. Sorren screamed through his teeth.

Lantern dropped a pouch on the table. "Guild's take for this week. Next time, double. Or we collect interest the old way."

Sorren nodded, holding his hand like it might fall off.

Stone gave the room one last look. No one met his eye.

"Let's go."

They stepped back into the mist. Smoke still hung low, clinging to stone and water like it didn't know where else to go.

A bell rang. Three times. Low. Flat.

Lantern asked, "What's that mean?"

Stone didn't answer.

Didn't like the shape of the air.

By the time they made it back to the wharfhouse, the street was too quiet. Fog still clung to the stones. Smoke still bled uphill. Stone didn't say much. Never did after a job. The others kept pace behind him, quiet as rope. Hookhand peeled off without a word. Seasnake muttered something about currents. Lantern lingered at the edge, eyes darting.

Stone pushed the door open.

Stopped.

Blood.

Old enough to be dark, fresh enough to catch the light. It had pooled, streaked, spattered. Spread across the floor in thick ropes, like someone had tried to clean it, then gave up. The smell was worse—metal, meat, smoke, rot. All the wrong kinds of memory.

He followed it back through the hallway.

Found the storeroom door cracked.

Inside—

He stood in the doorway for a long time.

Not a body. Not anymore. Just parts. Limbs torn where they shouldn't be. Bone where it didn't belong.

What was left of the Knife.

Stone stepped in. Quiet. Careful. Knees down, close to the mess. Looked at it, not like a mourner, but like a man trying to make sense of what couldn't be undone. Some of the cuts were clean. Others—weren't. None of it accidental. This wasn't a fight. This was work.

The Crooked Dagger was gone.

He looked around. Saw the prints. Barefoot. Light. Walking, not running. He exhaled. Long and slow. Didn't follow. Not yet.

Behind him, a voice. "Stone? Everything—?"

He didn't look back. "Get the others," he said. "No one leaves the docks. Not until I say."

Lantern didn't answer, but he left. Good enough.

Stone stood there a while. Took in the mess. The man who used to call himself The Knife—gone. Nothing left but blood and bad memory.

"Boss," he said. Not like a name. Just the last word in a hard ending.

Then he stepped outside. The fog was lifting, but the city wasn't any clearer. Somewhere out there was a boy with blood on his hands and a dagger no one should've held twice.

# Chapter 27.    The Quiet Crown

The Brass Griffin had escaped the worst of the fire. Its walls were stone, its bones old, and it stood far enough from Gallows Square to be spared by the flames. Still, the scent lingered — smoke baked into mortar, into cloth, into memory. Outside its doors, the city scraped itself into motion. Below, across the visible slope of Gatos, the burnt heart of the city pulsed with sound: hammers, shouts, carts groaning under rubble. Rebuilding had begun.

Aieria stood on the upper balcony of the converted salon, a floor she had claimed in the weeks after the trial. Once a row of storage rooms and servants' quarters, it now served as her strategic centre. The walls were painted pale cream, the floors redressed in quiet tile. There was a table for planning, a settee for receiving, and a cabinet that hid both wine and weapons.

She stood at the railing, looking out over the city; Indaros lounged beside her, eyes turned inward, watching the room behind. The sea wind teased loose a strand of her coiled hair, which she did not reach to fix. Her jacket was charcoal wool, dusk-blue at the trim, immaculate. Her boots were polished. Her gloves, soft leather, fit like second skin. She had dressed not for mourning, not even for command, but for herself — every piece chosen with care, not to impress, but to fit. To be hers. Her posture was straight, but not stiff: the balance of someone used to standing alone, too proud to lean.

The sky above was a pale, colourless stretch — thinned by ash, but clean now, swept clear by coastal wind. It smelled of salt and scorched wood. The kind of smell that lingered in your hair and coat, no matter how many times you tried to forget it.

She watched as a pair of masons argued beside a half-fallen arch — arms waving, voices too far away to hear, though their gestures spoke volumes. A cart rumbled past them, its wheels stuttering over broken stone, and beyond it, a stream of children ran barefoot through dust and ash, laughing as though joy were not only possible, but abundant. It was not beauty. It never would be. But there was a rhythm to the city's recovery, and something like grace in its insistence on moving forward. Gatos had always refused to die, no matter how many times it had been promised the courtesy.

From here, she could see what remained of the Gallows. Everything around it had been consumed, and so now it stood exposed — an unintentional monument. Blackened. Bent. Still tall.

Her foothold was tenuous, scattered — built not from any sanctioned authority, but from gaps and overlooked corners. The Brass Griffin was hers, its staff loyal in the ways that mattered. Gossip flowed through her like a tide: the low, important sort that travelled faster than coin. There were men who watched her and wondered. Men who thought she might yet become something. That was enough—for now.

Sargo had been burned—visibly, irrevocably. Half his face gone, his grip on the Red Knives shaken. But he still sat the chair, and the city still bent beneath the weight of his name. Bolter, once his instrument in the courts, had not fared so well. The High Exalted Judiciar of Gatos' Grand Tribunal had been made a fool—publicly, memorably—by the boy from the Slag. He had been stripped of robes, titles, protection. Sargo, ever pragmatic, had blamed him for the ruin of empire and flesh alike. She did not know exactly how Bolter had fallen. Only that no one spoke his name now, and those who had once bowed to him, now spat.

She had reached too early, and the city had bitten back. Power, here, was no coronation—it was a noose disguised in velvet. She was not marked. Not yet. But she was remembered. That was, in its way, more dangerous.

As Sargo diminished, Malren had risen. The Watch moved like a tightened fist, and the Marshal, with his battered honour and unshakable posture, had become its spine. She had sent him a note—brief, elegantly worded. It had said only that she was alive, and that he had not been forgotten. There had been no reply. But then, power did not always announce itself in return addresses.

Solivar still breathed. That, too, was inevitable. He had transformed her failure into a libretto before the ash cooled. The trial, the fire, the humiliations—woven into verse and carried on the wind. She had not seen him since. She imagined he would reappear when it suited him, dramatic as ever, demanding her applause. She would not give it. Though she might offer him wine.

And Kest. Kest had proposed to Lady Iseth Val'Asara, Jewel of Tahl'Vareth, as if affection were a deed of title. He had placed his fortune, his ships, and his dangerous patience at her feet, and she had said nothing. She did not know what answer she would give. Only that she was not yet finished becoming whatever came next.

And Pip? Pip was gone.

Gone like smoke. Gone like the scorched heart of the city. His absence was the smoking hole at Gatos' centre—vacant, but the one thing no one could stop seeing. The loudest kind of emptiness. She didn't know what he'd become, only that she still saw him—small, broken, aflame—in every sudden silence. A figure haloed in ruin.

She did not thank God for his absence. She did not put her faith in God anymore. Only consequence.

She had once imagined reclaiming this city through theatre. Through law. Through precision. Now it stood gutted, its players scattered, the script burned.

She had failed. That was truth. The trial had gone on. The system had held. The city had burned and chosen to remain precisely what it was.

But she was still standing—burned, diminished, humiliated—but upright still. Not untouched, never that. Power had never spared her; it had stripped her, and left her wrapped in the only garment she had never shed: survival.

She heard the door open—a gentle, well-oiled sound, like a sigh from the past. There was a pause, deliberate and expectant. Kael had always entered rooms with a sort of silent authority, as though the walls ought to acknowledge him before the people did.

Indaros stiffened.

She did not turn. Her hands rested on the iron railing of the balcony; fingers poised like a pianist's in a moment of stillness. The air smelled of salt and cinders, but the sky had cleared to a pale and blameless blue. Below, the city murmured—a rhythm of hammers and wheel ruts, of merchants calling and children chasing shadows. Gallows Square lay in view, oddly tranquil in its ruin, ringed now by scaffolding and the purposeful flutter of workmen's sleeves.

"You moved too fast," he said, his voice clipped, as if the wind might carry it away.

She let her chin lift, eyes tracing a pair of pigeons

spiralling above the rooftops. "The city was burning," she replied, her tone as even as the breeze.

"That wasn't the plan."

Now she turned.

Kael stood just inside the threshold, framed in the golden spill of afternoon light. His eyes flicked toward her, then down — just once, quickly — as if to suppress a thought he had no use for. His coat, once immaculate, bore dust and a long fray at the hem. His boots were travel-worn. His face, unchanged in its severity, bore the weariness of someone who had witnessed too much and spoken too little.

"I didn't know there was still a plan," she said, not unkindly.

He took a step forward. Not with menace — Kael never postured — but with the deliberate weight of someone preparing to challenge a foundation.

Indaros moved. He stepped between them, not quickly, but with a certainty that made Kael stop short. The motion was fluid — defensive, not aggressive. A single hand hovered at his side, just near the hilt of his blade.

Kael's expression did not change. He only held Indaros' gaze.

"You were sent to protect her. Not to become her shield."

"I protect her. She earned it."

There was a long moment. The air between them felt charged—not with violence, but with recognition. Kael considered him for a breath, then nodded. Not agreement. Not approval. Just acceptance.

Aieria let the confrontation pass like weather—brief, unsettling, already moving on. She gave Indaros a small wave. The point was made. The weapon had shifted hands.

Kael stepped beside her, gaze sweeping over the broken city.

"You dismantled the Guild's theatre. Shattered the Grand Tribunal. Lost an asset we didn't yet fully understand. Set fire to the city's machinery."

Aieria's smile was small and without apology. "And yet—here we are."

He studied her for a moment, his brow knit, as if trying to reconcile the woman before him with the girl he'd once installed behind careful curtains.

"You should have died," he said.

She gave a slight shrug. The smile stayed, held in place like a brooch—ornamental, deliberate.

"You've changed."

"No," she could reply. "I've only stopped asking for

permission."

Kael's gaze drifted across the salon—its restored elegance, its symmetry, the unfussed strength of it. He looked past her, through the tall window, where the square continued to rise from ash and ruin.

"What did you do?" he asked. Not angrily. Not admiringly. Simply the question of a man confronting a new reality.

She did not answer at once. She crossed to the sideboard, uncorked the wine with quiet precision, and poured a single measure into a clean glass. She offered it to him like a title—slow, deliberate, her fingers brushing the glass as if passing a name too heavy to speak. Kael accepted it. Sipped. The silence that followed was not cold, but watchful.

Then she met his eyes, calm and unflinching.

"I survived," she said, as if it were the most natural thing in the world.

And it was.

On the third day after the square burned, the girl came selling nettle-dust pies down by the Hollow. Said her uncle had a bad leg, the Watch took her cart, and the baker's guild frowned on rogue pies, but she had stories for sale and those kept better than meat.

"You want the one with the boy and the gallows?" she asked, plucking lint from her sleeve like a noble with nowhere to be. "Or the queen who walks in smoke?"

The old woman chose the queen. Always the queen. Truth's got nothing to do with favourites.

"They say she never screamed," the girl whispered, pressing a pie into the woman's hands like it was consecrated. "Not when they hung her lover. Not when they named her ghost."

She crouched, carved a lopsided crown in the dust, and added a smirk—quick, crooked, like punctuation left by a thief.

"They say she lives under the old court now. With knives for servants. A dagger that drinks lies. A proper throne of bones, or maybe a chair nicked from a tavern, no one agrees."

A boy with knuckles like broken promises muttered, "Liar. She burned. My da saw it."

"Then your da's a fool with ash for eyes. She walks

still. And she's got a list."

Another girl hummed something low and sharp, the kind of tune that stabs you if you hum it wrong. A butcher's song. The rest picked it up, quiet first, then louder:

> *Where doth Aieria roam?*
> *Not in the sky, no more —*
> *She walks where saints forget to kneel,*
> *And names fall to the floor.*

By dusk they'd scattered—pie crumbs, song fragments, rumour trailing after them like perfume in a brothel hallway. But the crown stayed in the dust. Smudged by boots. Half a memory. Exactly the way stories like to be. And the wind—never clean—just the sort that fondles shutters and picks pockets, with the manners of a drunk and the memory of a knife, caught the song like a pickpocket catching a purse. It wound round rooftops and spires, bent round corner shrines like it was late for prayer, and twirled across the gallows scaffold like a bard late to rehearsal. Then it dropped. Deep. Down where the city forgets its name. Where rats have politics and corpses remember names. Where something that had once been a boy— or a curse, or a song, or all three— listened.

And grinned.

Because the wind, being no fool, knew a good story when it heard one.

# POSTSCRIPT

### Where Doth Aieria Roam?

*Where doth Aieria roam?*
*Not in the sky, no more —*
*She walks where saints forget to kneel,*
*And names fall to the floor.*

*They say she crossed the silver sea,*
*Her veil the salt and foam;*
*The Varikon Isles remember queens,*
*Though none dare call her home.*

*Or south, where dusked Tahl'Vareth dreams,*
*Where memory barters breath —*
*A ghost in silks that whisper flame,*
*Too bright for certain death.*

*Some say she haunts the forest paths*
*Where Durn keeps counsel grim —*
*A crooked blade beneath her cloak,*
*And lullabies grown dim.*

*She does not beg, she does not plead,*
*She does not wear a crown —*
*But streets remember how she walked,*
*And demons pulled her down.*

*Where doth Aieria roam?*
*Not in the sky, no more —*
*She walks where oaths were sold for coin,*
*And crowns rot on the floor*
.

— As sung in alleys, whispered in courts, and never

the same twice.